K19 SECURITY SOLUTIONS
TEAM TWO

—BOOK TWO—

MONK'S
FIRE

USA TODAY BESTSELLING AUTHOR
HEATHER SLADE

MONK'S FIRE

© 2019 Heather Slade

This book is a work of fiction. The names, characters, places and incidents are products of the writer's imagination or have been used fictitiously and are not to be construed as real. Any resemblance to persons, living or dead, actual events, locale or organizations is entirely coincidental.

Paperback:
979-8-88649-120-3

MORE FROM AUTHOR HEATHER SLADE

Table of Contents

Prologue

—Monk—
December

The ICU nurses were used to me showing up each morning without saying a word to anyone and then leaving the same way. So, like every other day of the last twenty-three, I walked past the desk silently when I left to get some dinner. Sure, it was Christmas, but I really didn't give a shit about holidays, especially this year, with my friend in intensive care.

When I got off the elevator on the main floor, I buttoned up the peacoat that had belonged to my grandfather, put on my beanie, and pulled it down over my ears. I reached into my pockets, took out my gloves, and put the left one on first. I was about to put on the right when I felt my cell phone vibrate. I got it out and swiped the screen.

Look up, it said; I did.

"Hi," said the woman who'd sent it, slowly approaching me.

"Saylor." Given I was unable to decide whether to tell her how good it was to see her or ask her what in the hell she was doing there, I said nothing more than her name.

"Merry Christmas, Monk."

"What are you doing here?"

"My mom, the girls, and I are spending Christmas in Annapolis again this year."

Last year, I'd been with Saylor and her family at the same place. One of the founding partners of K19 Security Solutions, a private security and intelligence firm where I was a junior partner, had hosted a Christmas celebration. Not only had I been there, but Onyx had too.

"How is he?" Saylor asked, as though she knew what I was thinking.

"No change."

"I'm sorry, Monk. I was praying for a Christmas miracle."

I eased the glove off my left hand, put them both in my pocket, and then stepped forward. I gripped Saylor's nape with one hand, wrapped my other arm around her waist, and kissed her. It wasn't a chaste kiss. I didn't waste time with shit like that. Not with her. I tightened my hold so Saylor's body was flush with mine and deepened our kiss.

I pulled back and looked in her eyes. "I'm sorry—"

She put her fingertips on my lips. "Don't."

No one was ever as easy on me as Saylor. And no one deserved to be hard on me more than she did.

"Where were you going?"

"Dinner."

She tucked her arm in mine. "Good. I'm hungry."

My loft was a ten-minute walk from the hospital. If I were alone, I'd stop and eat somewhere on the way.

"It's cold."

"I'm okay to walk," she said, snuggling up against me when we went outside.

In the almost year and a half since I met Saylor, we'd been apart far more than together, and yet she was able to read me like no one else ever had. Two words, and she knew what I was asking. It always surprised me, but it shouldn't.

"This is nice," she said when I opened the door to my loft and invited her in.

"Thanks." I'd gotten the three-bedroom unit because I wanted to be on the top floor of the building, and I wanted a view. I didn't care about it being too big for me or about the price.

When the listing agent offered to throw in the staging furniture for a nominal fee, I took her up on it. Everything else in it, I'd ordered online. I didn't have time to shop, not that I would've anyway. I spent every day at George Washington University Hospital, waiting for my friend to come out of the coma he'd been in since surviving a plane crash almost a month ago.

I took Saylor's coat and hung it in the closet with mine and then walked into the kitchen and opened the fridge. I kept it well stocked, again by ordering online and having the groceries delivered.

Saylor came up behind me and wrapped her arms around my waist. "When did you last eat?" she asked.

"Lunch. You said you were hungry."

"I can wait."

I closed the refrigerator door and led her into the master bedroom.

— Saylor —

Sex with Monk had always been incendiary. From the first time and every time since. I'd never been with another man who lit me on fire the way Monk did. It was as though an electrical current ran from every part of his body and traveled directly through my bloodstream whenever and however he touched me.

I watched as he undressed, like I always did. There was no pretense with this man as he unbuttoned his white dress shirt, revealing so much that I didn't know where to look first.

Around his thick neck, he wore four chains, each increasing in length. The first was an Aztec medallion on a thin piece of leather. I walked closer and fingered it, remembering the first time he'd explained its meaning.

"It's a *tonalpohualli*," he'd said. "It's a divination tool, keeping the delicate equilibrium of the divine forces residing inside of me."

The next was black braided leather with what looked to me like black onyx resting in patterned silver.

"Is this new?" I asked, running my fingertip over the black beads.

"It is."

"For Onyx?"

"Yes."

I walked my fingers lower, to the next—a blue-beaded rosary I'd seen before, but I didn't remember the silver cross that hung from it.

Last was the thick platinum chain from which hung a simple wedding ring that he'd told me had belonged to his mother.

The Aztec sun tattoo covering his right pec was one my brother, Razor, had too. It symbolized a belief in an afterlife. The ink continued in a sleeve of intricate symbols that abruptly ended at Monk's wrist. His other pec and shoulder were bare, as was his back, but the same ink that covered his right forearm, covered his left.

Monk eased the shirt off his arms and shoulders, revealing his thick, dark chest hair that narrowed as it trailed down his stomach.

When I unfastened the heavy copper buckle on his jeans, Monk grasped my small wrist in his big hand and stopped me.

"Wait, Saylor. We need to talk."

Talk? If there was anything Monk didn't do, it was talk. "Okay," I said, backing up to sit on the end of the bed.

Part 1

1

—Saylor—

Two Augusts Ago

"Okay, you two," I said to my brother and his girlfriend, Ava. "The girls are tired, so I'm taking them home—"

"What?" Razor asked, following my line of sight.

"Who is that?"

"Monk. He's hangin' with us for a few days."

"Someone you work with?"

"Yep."

"He's kinda hot."

"He doesn't talk very much," said Ava. "I think I've heard him say a total of three words."

"Is that why you call him Monk?"

Razor nodded.

"I can live with that, as long as he's not celibate too."

My brother raised an eyebrow, which I would've given him shit about if the girlfriend wasn't with him. After all, this was the first time I'd met her.

"Anyway, we're goin' home. Invite me back over sometime to meet the monk." I turned around to look for my girls and saw both had gotten back into the ocean's freezing water. Off the coast of Oregon, the water's temp rarely got above sixty degrees even in the summer.

"What the heck," I muttered, joining them. They'd end up putting their ice-cold feet on me anyway, so I might as well lower my body temperature to theirs.

My two girls, Sierra and Savannah, looked like twins, but they were actually a year apart, like Razor and I were. Savannah, my six-year-old, was almost taller than her older sister, and it drove my seven-year-old crazy.

Both were blonde, blue-eyed towheads, like their father had been when he was a little boy. I had dark-brown hair that looked almost black, and dark eyes. No one ever asked if they were my daughters. Maybe they just assumed I was the babysitter—until one of them called me Mama.

As I tiptoed into the water, I looked over my shoulder and saw the man my brother called Monk standing where he had been before. The fact that he didn't talk much didn't bother me. I wasn't interested in him for conversation, at least from what I could see from a distance. And I definitely wasn't interested in a relationship.

I'd done that, failed miserably, and did my best to raise the two little girls who were a product of that relationship, all on my own. The liar-cheater-beater bastard, as I referred to my ex, hadn't been in our lives for almost five years, and if he ever showed up again, a restraining order would keep him at least one hundred yards away from me and my girls. That is, if he ever got out of the white-collar prison my brother made sure he got locked away in.

His lying and cheating had been going on for years, I found out after his arrest. He didn't lie only to me; he'd swindled a lot of people in the community out of a great deal of money via a Ponzi scheme similar to Bernie Madoff's.

As far as cheating on me, he'd been smart enough not to do it in Yachats where we both knew practically everyone. However, after our divorce, people told me they'd seen him with other women in several of the small towns that dotted the Oregon coastline.

The final nail in the coffin of our marriage came the day he'd hit me. I didn't hesitate to call my brother as

I held my one- and two-year-old girls on each arm and ran from the house.

In the back of my mind, I knew two things. One, he wouldn't strike me when I was carrying the babies, and two, the woman who lived next door and spent all her time sitting near her picture window, watching both the ocean and the neighborhood happenings, would call the cops in a heartbeat if she saw the bastard come after me.

"Cliff hit me. I'm on my way to you, and I'm putting you on speaker," I'd said to Razor, stuffing my cell phone inside my bra so he'd hear anything that happened if it turned out I was wrong about my ex coming after me.

The girls and I moved in with Razor that day and lived with him for the six months it took for my divorce to be finalized, and then another year after that. It had taken me that much time to feel like I was ready to let go of my fear and start living again.

Razor bought a duplex two doors down from his house, and that's where our mom, the girls, and I now lived.

I shook my head, willing the bad memories to skedaddle like my sweet girls and I were about to do. I looked over my shoulder one more time, but the hotter-than-shit guy wasn't there.

—Monk—

I walked back inside the house but couldn't take my eyes off the pretty woman on the beach. She had to be related to Razor; she looked just like him.

She had long dark hair and the same crisp, angular facial features her brother had. From where I stood, her skin looked like porcelain. Not pale, just flawless. Her body looked lean in the one-piece black bathing suit she wore, but she had the kind of breasts I loved. Not too big, not too small.

She looked up at me more than once, and as tempted as I was to walk down to the beach and meet her, that wasn't why I was in Yachats, Oregon.

My job was to protect Ava McNamara from the sons of bitches who'd kidnapped her twin sister and two of their friends, and who Razor believed wanted Ava dead. If it became necessary, I'd lay my life on the line to protect her, without hesitation.

This was the work I'd been trained to do, and it was the only kind of job I'd ever wanted—to protect the innocent and kill the bad guys, like the ones who'd killed my sister right before her eighteenth birthday.

I was eleven at the time, skinny, scrawny, and unable to protect her from the men who came in to rob our house but found her instead. They'd raped her first and then shot her.

They'd shot me too, but unlike her, I'd lived. I made a vow that day to dedicate my life to protecting those unable to protect themselves, and I'd lived it every day since.

I didn't remember a whole lot about the years immediately following my sister's death, other than that vow. My mother told me that I didn't talk for close to two years, and even when I started again, I said as little as possible. Now, it wasn't something I thought about; I spoke when I had something to say; otherwise, I didn't.

A week before I retired from active duty with the Marine Corps, my commander at the time arranged for me to meet Doc Butler, K19's original founder. We'd had dinner, and by its end, I knew what I'd be doing once my retirement was official. I was headed straight to The Farm, as it was known, where I'd undergo training to become a CIA agent.

In that role, I'd gone undercover more times than I could count. During one of my assignments, my mother died. It was the only thing I hated about the job I did. The mission came first, no matter what.

Working for Doc's company was different, though. K19's policies weren't as strict as the company's. If someone needed time off, they got it. I hadn't yet, but I appreciated it when I saw the other men and women I worked with take time for their families.

I went downstairs to finish the workout I'd started earlier. When I heard Razor and Ava come inside a while later, I went upstairs to check in.

"Am I interrupting?" I asked when I met them in the kitchen.

"Not at all. I was about to make eggs and toast, if you'd like to join us."

I walked over and opened the refrigerator, pulling things out and setting them on the counter. Plain eggs and toast didn't really appeal to me.

"I could make omelets if you'd like," I offered.

"You cook?" Razor asked.

"I spent a year undercover as a private chef."

"I can't cook for shit," said Razor, turning to Ava. "Do you think you could manage an omelet, or would you prefer to stick with plain eggs?"

"I'd love an omelet. Thanks, Monk," Ava answered.

"Damn, you're a good cook," Razor said, rubbing his stomach when he finished eating.

"Chef."

"Oh, sorry. Maybe we should start calling you that instead."

"Chef Monk is fine with me."

"So, Monk. Are you single?" asked Ava.

"Excuse me?"

"You know…not married, not dating anyone."

I looked at Razor and then back at Ava.

"Yeah. Single."

"Are you gonna ask him anything else, or just leave him hangin'?" Razor asked.

"I wasn't sure I should."

"My sister has the hots for you, Monk. Beware, though. She comes with two of the sweetest little girls on the face of the earth."

I didn't say anything. A minute later, I went back into the kitchen.

"Hey, you cooked; I'll clean up," Razor shouted over to me when I started rinsing the dishes.

"I got it," I answered. "Your sister. Was she the one here earlier?"

"Yep."

"She's pretty."

"My mom's gotta be chomping at the bit to have us over for dinner. We'll get Saylor to bring the girls, and we'll bring you along with us."

"Saylor? That's her name?"

"Yep."

"Cool name," I said before I turned back to the dishes.

"I can help," Ava offered, joining me near the sink.

"I like doing dishes. It relaxes me."

"You should invite your sister back over now," Ava said to Razor. "A man who cooks the way Monk does who also likes doing dishes? She should grab him before someone else does."

I didn't see where Razor and Ava went when they left the room, and I didn't care. I was happy to be alone. I wasn't lying when I said doing dishes relaxed me. Cooking did too, as long as it wasn't a job, like it had been when I went undercover as a chef.

That mission had been to take down a Boston crime syndicate, and it had taken almost a year for my team to gather the evidence to do it. I'd worked as a private chef for the ringleader and lost count of how many times I'd wanted to poison the bastard while the investigation was taking place.

Eventually, we nailed him, he turned state's evidence, and we took down a whole helluva lot more of the bad guys.

After I finished the dishes and cleaned up the rest of the kitchen, I poured myself a glass of the cognac I found in one of the kitchen cupboards. I went outside, watched the sun go down over the Pacific Ocean, and thought about Razor's pretty sister.

"Ava and I are going for a run," Razor said the next morning.

"North or south?"

"North."

"Roger that."

They weren't gone long when I got a call from Doc with intel indicating that Ava was being tracked.

"What's up? We were just about to head back," said Razor when I called his cell.

I repeated the intel I'd been given.

"Fuck," Razor spat under his breath. *"Shit.* It wasn't my imagination. We need cover, Monk. Someone's following us. There's a four-wheeler in the garage."

"Roger that," I responded. "I've got your coordinates; I'm on my way."

I'd just pulled out of the garage when I received another call, this time from one of K19's on-staff pilots.

"We've got drone coverage on Razor and Ava," said Onyx.

"Didn't know you were here."

"I've been on standby with the plane. I got the call to jump in on Ava's detail right after you did."

I arrived at the beach parking lot at the same time Onyx did in the SUV.

Hang tight, Onyx messaged me.

I sat nearby on the four-wheeler until I saw that Ava and Razor were in the SUV before going back to the house to await further instructions.

2

—Saylor—

I'd just made lunch for the girls and sat down for the first time all morning when my cell phone rang. I thought about not answering, but I wasn't that person. Even if it was from a number I didn't know, I still picked up. Razor had warned me that doing so wasn't smart, but my curiosity always won out.

This time, the call was from a number I did recognize.

"Hey, sis."

"Hey, Raze. What's up? Why are you at Dad's cabin?"

"I need your help with something."

He asked me to make contact with Monk and gave me a cell number. "Tell him I need two phones. He'll understand what to do."

"Roger that," I joked. "Anything else?"

"I'm not sure how long we'll be here. We might need some provisions." Razor rattled off a list.

"Be there as soon as I can."

I went next door and found my mother out on the deck, watering pots of flowers.

"Hey, sweetie."

"I just got a call from Raze. He needs me to bring some stuff to Dad's fishing cabin."

My mother raised her eyebrows like I'd expected her to.

"He's there with Ava."

Another eyebrow raise.

"Anyway, he gave me a list of things he needs. Wanna come along?"

She practically dropped the watering can where she stood, wiped her hands on her shorts, and came out of the gate.

I laughed. "Do you want to lock up the house?"

"That's a good idea." She went back inside, and I went to get my girls.

"When can we visit Aunt Ava again?" asked Sierra when I came back in.

"How's right now?"

Both girls squealed and jumped from their chairs.

"What's this?" asked my mom, coming in the front door.

"Aunt Ava! Aunt Ava!" the girls sang.

"They've been begging me to take them to see her all morning."

"This should be interesting."

"Stop raising your eyebrows. You'll get wrinkles," I said, reaching out to smooth the skin on her forehead.

"More wrinkles, you mean."

"Oh, *shit*. I have to call Monk. Be right back."

I went into the bedroom, escaping my girls' cries that I owed them both money for swearing.

"Yeah, yeah," I muttered as I dialed the number Razor had given me.

"Perrin."

"Uh, Monk? This is Saylor Davis, um, Razor's sister."

"I know who you are."

"Right. He asked me to call and tell you that he needs two phones and some clothes for Ava. He said you'd understand."

"Where?"

"He didn't say. He's at my dad's fishing cabin. Maybe he wants you to take them there."

"I'll get back to you."

I stared at the phone; he'd ended the call. When Ava said the man didn't say three words to her, she wasn't kidding. Evidently, goodbye wasn't necessary. A minute later, I got a text with GPS coordinates. I plugged them into my map app and saw it was for the beach club our family belonged to. My phone pinged again, this time with a locker number.

"Let's go," I said, coming out of the bedroom, but neither my daughters nor their grandmother were anywhere in sight. I locked up the house and went out the door to the garage, where I found the three of them waiting in my Jeep.

"Anxious much?" I muttercd.

I drove to the beach club first and found a duffel bag inside the locker with the right number. When I came back out, I looked for Monk—not that I would've stopped to talk; just laying eyes on him would've been enough.

"I thought we were going to see Aunt Ava," whined Sierra from the back seat when I climbed into the Jeep.

"We are, but first she asked us to stop and pick up some very important things for her. She knew she could count on the two of you to help her. Was she right?"

With wide eyes, both girls nodded their heads.

I made two more stops before driving inland to the cabin where my father used to take Razor and me fishing. I doubted my mother had been here since my dad died.

"Are you okay?" I asked, reaching over to squeeze her hand.

"I'm fine, sweetie."

Razor walked out the front door just as we drove up.

"Where's Ava?" I asked, climbing out of the Jeep.

"Uh…she's calling me Razor again."

I laughed, knowing she only called him that when she was pissed; otherwise, she called him Tabon, his given name.

"I need help," Razor whispered.

"Aunt Ava is sleeping," I said to the girls, putting a finger to my lips. "Why don't you and Ya-Ya take a walk down to the lake. When you get back, she'll probably be awake."

"Okay," both girls grumbled, taking their grandmother's hands.

"All right, they're gone. Tell me what happened. Word for word."

After Razor reiterated their conversation, I left my brother sitting on the porch and went inside to see if I could smooth things over with Ava.

We'd only been talking a few minutes when I heard a knock. Razor stuck his head inside. "Can I come in?" he asked.

I quickly excused myself, went back outside, and sat on the porch. I closed my eyes, remembering a time when Razor and I came to the cabin with our dad when we were teenagers.

It had started out as a shitty day. My dad had picked a fight with my mom and then hustled Razor and me into his Jeep, the same one I still drove.

As we got closer to the cabin that day, it was as though the tension in the car simply faded away.

We ended up having a great day and caught lots of fish. When we trudged up to the cabin, my mom was there too, and it was as though the earlier argument had never happened.

"Ava will be out shortly," Razor said when he came out and sat down next to me.

"Good."

"How's Ya-Ya?" he asked.

"She's okay. I don't think she's been up here since Dad died."

"Who has been?"

"Me. I bring the girls up here sometimes. I want them to know things about him, ya know?" I sighed, looked toward the lake, and saw my mom and the girls walking back up.

Before they got to the cabin, Ava came outside.

"Aunt Ava!" Both girls shouted and came running, dragging their grandmother with them.

I leaned back on my hands and watched the look on my brother's face as Ava talked to them. He was absolutely head over heels in love with this woman.

I envied that, but not enough to ever go down that road again. I'd learned my lesson; love worked out for some people, but not for me.

When Razor got up and walked over to the picnic table, I followed.

"Thanks for getting the phones, sis."

"You're welcome. Although you should thank Monk, or maybe I should." I wiggled my eyebrows. "I'll go rescue Ava from my girls, who are now probably asking to get fitted for flower girl dresses for your wedding."

Razor was distracted entering codes into the phones but looked up. "Wait. What? My wedding?"

I punched him and walked away.

"I am seriously outnumbered," Razor said, walking over to the picnic table where Ava was still chatting with the girls and their grandmother.

"You could invite Monk to join us," I suggested.

"He already did," said Monk, walking out of the woods and scaring the shit out of me.

"I told him we needed a cook," said Razor.

"Chef."

"Right. Mom, meet Monk. He's a chef, and Saylor has a mad crush on him," said my brother.

"Monk, this is my mom, Sally."

After shaking my mom's hand, Monk turned toward me and winked. "I already know who you are," he said, repeating his words from our phone call.

I couldn't help myself—I put my hand on my heart. Mouthing "Oh my God" at Razor, I didn't even attempt to hide it from anyone, including Monk.

—*Monk*—

"You're pretty," I said to Razor's sister as I took a drink from my insulated water bottle.

"So are you."

I looked over at the two girls. "Razor says they're yours."

"That's right."

I turned my head back toward her. "They don't look anything like you."

"I used to have blonde hair just like theirs."

"Really?"

She laughed. "Hell no. Do I look like I used to have blonde hair?"

I shook my head; she was smirking. She'd caught me off guard, and not many people did. I liked it.

"Heard their dad's in prison."

"That's good to hear," said Saylor as she reached over, took the water bottle from my hand, and brought it to her lips. "I don't keep track."

I looked into her dark-brown eyes. She had smile lines at the corners. I liked that too. I looked down the length of her, not hiding that I was. I took my water bottle back and had another drink.

When I felt my cell vibrate, I handed the water back to her and pulled out my phone. I read the text and looked over at Razor.

"I hate to cut the party short, but we need to leave," he said without me needing to say a word.

Saylor stood, as did her mother. "Time to go, girls." She hustled her daughters toward Ava, and they hugged goodbye.

"Monk will grab your bag when you're ready," Razor said to Ava after the others had left.

I followed her inside and was in the process of checking each room when something outside caught my eye. I went through the kitchen and out the back door.

Before I could get a word out to warn Razor or Ava, someone hit me from behind with what felt like a sledgehammer. As I fell to the ground, blood trickled down the side of my face. I floated in and out of consciousness, but saw three men carrying Ava out and running into the woods, right before everything went black.

3

—Saylor—

When we got home, the girls went inside to play while my mom and I sat outside on the porch.

"I hate this part. Waiting for word," I said.

"I do too."

While neither of us knew the details about what my brother actually did for a living, when he'd disappear for weeks or sometimes months on end, we both knew enough to glean that Ava was in danger and that was why we'd had to leave so abruptly.

"What did you think of her?" I asked.

"The girls like her. That's always a good sign." My mother was looking out at the sea. While moments ago, we were both worried about Razor, talking about Ava being in his life seemed to give us both a sense of peace.

"I like her too."

"Your brother's in love."

I met my mother's gaze. "Picked up on that, huh?"

We both smiled.

"I'll admit, I worried it would never happen."

"What about you, sweetheart? When will you open your heart again?"

I stood, walked over to the deck's railing, and looked out at the ocean. This was a conversation we'd had more than once. "Never again, Mom."

She came and stood beside me. She covered my hand with hers. "It's time, Saylor."

"As you can see, I don't have suitors lined up waiting."

"Monk seemed interested."

"Interested and lining up to woo me are two different things. Plus, he works with Razor."

"Right." She pointed out at the ocean to the pod of whales that, instead of migrating, lived year-round off the coast of Yachats.

Like her, I never took being able to see the beautiful creatures for granted. It was one of the things I liked best about the small town I'd lived in since I was born.

I'd gone to college in Eugene for aeronautical engineering, in part because it was funded by the NASA Oregon Space Grant, and I thought that was the coolest thing ever.

When I graduated with a bachelor's degree, I came straight back to Yachats. In hindsight, I should've started flight training right away and continued my pursuit of becoming a pilot. Instead, I'd gotten married.

I always struggled with wishing I'd done things differently and the idea that if I had, the two beautiful little girls who made my soul shine wouldn't grace the planet.

"Monk said Cliff is still in prison."

"Good to know."

"That's what I said."

"What else is bothering you?" my mom asked.

Even though I'd done nothing wrong, the idea that Monk knew my ex-husband was an abuser, embarrassed me.

"I thought you were over feeling guilty about something you couldn't control, Saylor."

"I don't feel guilty. I feel stupid."

My mom shook her head. "It's a waste of time, and you know it. Should I call myself stupid because of the things your father did?"

This was a conversation we'd had several times in the last five years. Each time, I'd say it was different and my mom would remind me it wasn't different at all. This time, I didn't bother arguing.

When my cell phone rang two days later, a feeling of foreboding washed over me even before I answered it.

"This is Monk Perrin calling."

Instinctively, I knew something was wrong. "What's happened?"

"Your brother was shot. He's in surgery."

I grabbed the closest chair and sat down, listening as Monk told me my brother's condition was critical.

"I've arranged for transportation to take you from your house to the airfield in Florence. From there, a private plane will bring you to Seattle. When it lands, someone will meet you to bring you to the hospital."

I called my best friend and made arrangements for the girls to stay with her, and then went next door to tell my mom.

Monk was waiting at the hospital's entrance when we arrived. "He's still in surgery. Come with me."

When I walked in and saw the looks on the faces of the men and women my brother worked with, I dissolved into tears.

Monk, still beside me, pulled me into his arms.

"I'm sorry," I said as he stroked my hair. "I don't even know you."

When I started to back away, he tightened his hold. "Sure, you do."

An hour later, two people, both wearing scrubs, came through the double doors.

"Are you Mr. Sharp's family?" one of them asked, approaching.

"I'm his mother," said my mom, grabbing my hand.

"Your son is on life support."

Monk had his arm around me, and my mom and I were still holding hands; I knew that much. Everything else, though, seemed to be happening in slow motion. People were talking, but I couldn't understand what they were saying.

"The doctor asked if you want to go see him," said Monk.

"Yes," I mumbled, but when he released me from his embrace, all I wanted to do was crawl back into it.

"Follow me," I heard a woman say to my mother.

"The coma he's in is medically induced," explained the man who introduced himself as the surgeon who had operated on Razor after a nurse took us through a set of double doors and into the ICU. "A ventilator is doing his breathing for him; everything else you see is monitoring his heart rate and blood pressure, as well as feeding him fluids."

I put my arm around my mother's shoulders when the nurse led us into his room. My mom gasped, and I tightened my grip, watching as she reached out to hold Razor's hand.

"He's warm," she said, looking up at me.

I walked around to the opposite side of the bed, sat in a chair, and held my brother's other hand.

"He's going to be okay, Mom," I said, not knowing whether he would be or not.

"Do either of you know who Avarie is?" the nurse asked.

"I do. Why?"

"He was asking for her when they brought him in."

"The people who were with us in the waiting area might be able to track her down." There was no way I could leave my brother's side after only being with him for less than a few minutes.

My mom brushed her fingers over Razor's forehead.

"He's going to be okay," I repeated after the nurse left. "Keep praying."

"I know he is," she murmured. "He just needs to hear Ava's voice."

"The doctor would like to talk with you both," said the nurse when she came back in a few minutes later.

"Come on, Mom," I said, helping her up.

The nurse led us down the hallway into another room. "He'll be right in," she said, closing the door behind her. A few minutes later, there was a soft knock on the door and a man we hadn't met before walked in.

"I'm Dr. Mason," he said.

"Do you know if anyone was able to find Ava?" my mom asked.

"The nurse said my brother was asking for her when they brought him in," I explained.

"Yes, I believe I heard someone say she's in with him now."

"Good," said my mom.

"I'm here to discuss your son's condition and talk to you about removing—"

I stood, almost knocking the chair over.

"Where are you going?"

"Ava should be here too." I rushed out of the room before my mom could stop me. I had to get the hell out of there before the doctor said another word.

When I got to Razor's room, the door was open and I could hear Ava talking to him.

"I love you so much. I have since the first time I saw you. And you love me too—Saylor told me you did—so you can't leave me."

When Ava broke down and sobbed, I eased the door open and rested my hand on her back.

"I'm so sorry," Ava cried, jumping up and hugging me.

"Shh," I soothed. "Come with me. There's someone I want you to talk to."

Ava turned to look at Razor.

"We'll come back." I took Ava's hand and led her to the room where Dr. Mason and my mom waited.

"Is this Avarie?" the doctor asked when we walked in.

"Yes, I'm Ava."

"Good." He looked up at me. "Now that you're both here, I'll tell you what I've just told Mrs. Sharp. Tabon's organs are all functioning, and we have significant brain activity, enough that we believe we can withdraw life support."

"Isn't that wonderful news?" my mom asked.

"He's going to be okay?" Ava whispered.

"I'm not going to lie." The doctor laced his fingers together. "His recovery may not be easy or quick, but yes, I believe he's going to be okay."

He turned back to my mom. "Would you like to be with him when we turn off life support?"

"Of course." She stood and reached for my hand. "Ava, would you like to be with us?"

Ava squared her shoulders and took my other hand. "If you don't mind, yes, I would."

The doctor led the three of us back down the hallway. "A respiratory therapist will be assisting me by disconnecting the tube from the machine. I'm confident Tabon will begin breathing on his own immediately."

"Are you sure you want to be here?" my mom asked. Both Ava and I nodded and followed her into the room.

My mom put her hand on Razor's arm and motioned for Ava and me to do the same.

They disconnected the tubing, and a split second later, my brother took a breath.

"Thank you, God," I whispered.

"Now, what happens?" my mom asked.

"We wait for him to wake up," the doctor answered.

"How long will that take?"

He shrugged. "That's up to him."

—Monk—

When Saylor and her mother were taken back to see Razor, I went in search of Gunner. The man wasn't just Razor's partner in K19; the two had been close friends for many years.

When I found him in the chapel, I quietly opened the door, dipped my finger in the holy water, and crossed myself before taking a seat next to Gunner.

I took the rosary from around my neck and handed it to him. "My mother held this and prayed when I was shot."

He held out his hand, and I rested the rosary on his palm.

"We're all praying," I said, standing to give him privacy.

Not long after I'd returned to the ICU waiting room, Ava came out.

"He's breathing on his own. We're just waiting for him to decide to open his eyes," she reported. "Where's Gunner?" she asked, looking around the room.

"In the chapel," I answered.

"Where is that?"

When someone else volunteered to take her to him, I stood to leave, but when Saylor and her mother came out of the double doors, I sat back down.

"He's breathing on his own." Saylor repeated Ava's words and then sat down next to me.

"That's good news."

"Thank you for being here," she said.

"Is there anything you need?"

Saylor scrubbed her face with her hand. "Mom and I are going to need a place to stay."

"I'll take care of it."

She rested her hand on my arm. "Thank you."

"One room or two?"

"Just one. Mom and I will share."

When I stood to leave, Saylor did too. "You're coming back, right?"

"Yes. I'm coming back."

"He's awake," she said when I came back an hour later. She walked over and stood in front of me close enough to touch. "I can't explain it, but I feel better when you're here. I hope you don't think—"

I put my fingers on her chin and looked into her eyes. "Do you believe in angels?"

"I guess I do."

"I had a sister. She's an angel now."

"I'm sorry, Monk."

"Sometimes I feel like she leads me where I need to be."

4

—Saylor—

"Are you ready to go, Mom?"

"I am, but you can stay if you want to."

"Monk made arrangements for us to have a room at the hotel connected to the hospital."

She looked over at him. "How thoughtful."

"I can walk over with you," he offered, leading us out of the ICU and down one floor to a bridge connecting the hospital to the hotel. As we walked, he kept his hand on the small of my back. I liked feeling it there.

When we got to the lobby, Monk pulled out a small envelope containing key cards. "Your room is on the tenth floor."

"Thank you. Are you leaving?"

"No. Doc booked every room on the floor."

"I didn't realize there were so many people here."

"There aren't."

I'd heard Razor say Doc was generous to a fault, and he wasn't complaining when he'd said it.

Monk led us to the elevator. "Have you eaten?" he asked while it took us to our floor.

"I don't remember the last time I ate."

"I can bring you something."

"That's very nice of you, Monk," said my mom. "You've done so much already."

"What do you like?" he asked, looking between us.

"It'll be easier if I go with you. Will you be all right, Mom?"

"Of course."

"I'll just get her settled."

"I'll wait here."

When I came back out, he was leaning up against the wall.

"Ready?"

He didn't answer, but walked next to me with his hand on the small of my back like he had earlier.

"I like that," I murmured.

"What's that?" he asked, pressing the call button.

"Feeling your hand on me."

"I like it too."

"Would you like a table, sir?" the *maître d'* asked when we arrived at the hotel's restaurant.

"Would you mind?" I asked, motioning toward the bar. "I could really use a drink."

After we were seated, Monk leaned forward, close enough that I could see the speckles of color in his eyes. "What would you like?" he asked.

"A glass of wine would be nice."

Monk opened the bar menu.

"Red, please," I added, hoping he wouldn't mind choosing for me.

"A glass of the Elk Cove Pinot Noir for the lady," he said when the bartender approached. "I'll have the same."

"Thank you, Monk. For everything," I said when the bartender walked away.

"What about Mrs. Sharp?" he asked.

"If you're referring to my mother, she'll tell you her name is Sally and Mrs. Sharp was her mother-in-law. And I can guarantee you that she is presently sound asleep. By the way, that wine is one of my favorites."

Monk nodded as though he already knew that. He reached over and brushed my hair from my face.

"You folks want to look at a menu?" the bartender asked, setting the glasses in front of us.

"Please," Monk responded.

I leaned against the padded bar stool, then picked up my glass and swirled it, inhaling deeply. "I love this wine," I said more to myself than to him.

He smiled, raised his glass, and took a drink.

"You're an enigma, Monk."

"Not intentionally."

"Ava said you didn't talk much."

"Not usually."

"I'm good with that."

He took another drink of his wine.

"I told her I didn't mind as long as you weren't celibate too."

Monk put his arm on the back of my stool and leaned in like he had before. "Not celibate."

"Thank God."

He brought his hand to my cheek. "I want to kiss you."

"I'd like that."

He moved his hand to my neck and brought his mouth to mine. When his tongue outlined my lower lip, I felt something hard and round on its tip.

"Your tongue is pierced," I gasped.

He smiled again.

"I like that."

He grinned and kissed me again. That alone was enough to heat my blood. Allowing myself to imagine how that piercing would feel as his tongue explored the rest of my body, brought it to a boil.

When the bartender cleared his throat, I pulled back and bit my bottom lip. Good Lord, this man was hot. I fanned my face.

"I feel it too," he murmured, making me flush even more.

I tried to bring the words on the menu into focus. "We should eat."

"We should."

"Room service?" I asked.

"What would you like?"

I couldn't concentrate enough to think. My eyes met Monk's, and he studied me before turning to the bartender.

"We'll start with the beet and Dungeness salad. Followed by the rigatoni amatriciana and the New York strip, medium-rare."

"Certainly. Any sides with that?"

I shook my head. "Not for me."

Monk stood. "Room 1012," he said. "Add a bottle of the Stonestreet Meritage to the order."

"Anything else?" the bartender asked.

"Please have the oven-roasted chicken brought to room 1014."

"With a bottle of still water to each," I added.

Monk signed for the check and took my hand in his.

"We're in room 1014," I said as we walked to the elevator.

"Your mother is in room 1014."

"And you're next door."

"We're next door."

—Monk—

Once we were in the elevator and alone, I backed Saylor up against the wall and held both of her wrists behind her back with one hand. I leaned my body against hers.

"What are you doing?" she asked.

"I want to kiss you."

"What's stopping you?"

I brought my mouth to hers, kissing her deeply until I heard the ping of the elevator door opening. I led her down the hall to my room.

"The key card is in the pocket of my shirt. If this is what you want, take it out."

Saylor pulled it out, held it up to the reader, and the door sprung open. I followed her inside and kicked the door closed behind us, impatiently ravishing her mouth again.

"Sit there," I told her, pointing to the end of the bed.

I pulled my shirt out from where it was tucked into my jeans and unbuttoned it.

When she began to unbutton hers, I told her to stop. She froze and stared up at me. "I want to do it."

She dropped her hands to her sides and trailed her eyes from my face and down my body as each bit of it was uncovered. When I was naked, she slowly trailed them back up.

I pushed her back on the bed, unfastened her jeans, and pulled them off along with her panties. After spreading her legs, I stood between them and took her hands in mine. I pulled her to a sitting position and, starting at the top, unbuttoned her blouse.

When she shrugged it from her shoulders, I reached around and unfastened her pink lace bra and tossed it on the floor.

I knelt then and attacked her nipples, soothing each bite by rolling the silver ball at the end of my tongue around the hardened buds. "Put your hands at your sides," I said when I felt her fingers in my hair.

"I want to touch you," Saylor whined.

"You will."

When I rolled the silver ball on her clit, she shuddered. When I thrust two fingers inside her, she came.

"Remember earlier when I said I liked your piercing? I was wrong. I love it," she said without opening her eyes.

I stretched out next to her on the bed and rolled to my back, pulling her until she was lying on top of me.

"I like feeling your body on mine," I said, stroking her back. "Since the first time I saw you, I've wanted to run my fingers over your porcelain skin."

She lifted her head and kissed me. "I want more of you."

"Take it, Saylor."

She positioned her knees on either side of my body and straddled my stomach.

"Do you…have any…"

"In my wallet."

She slowly slid lower, kissing her way down my body like I'd done to her.

"Either take me in your mouth or get the condom."

When she chose the former, I closed my eyes and focused solely on the pleasure she gave.

I wanted to weave my fingers in her silky hair, but rested my arms at my sides, like I'd told her to do. The gift she was giving me was too good to do anything but accept.

The knock came at the door just as Saylor was kissing her way back up my sated body. I grabbed her arms before she could get up, brought my mouth close to hers, and kissed her. When whoever it was knocked again, I turned my head. "Leave it in the hallway," I shouted toward the door.

Saylor smiled.

I released my grip on her arms. "Put the condom on me." She did and then straddled me. With my hands on her waist, I eased her down on my cock.

"Oh God," she groaned, arching her back until I was in as deep as I could get. I covered both her breasts with my hands, toying with her nipples.

I pulled myself up so I could reach them with my mouth. "I want to pierce these," I said, flicking her nipples with my tongue. I gripped the cheeks of her ass and began moving her back and forth, setting my own rhythm.

"Link your ankles behind my back," I said, taking control of her body and mine. I thrust hard and then backed off when I felt her on the brink. I did that again and again until she begged me not to stop.

"Say it again," I demanded.

"God, Monk, please don't stop. I'm begging you."

"Give it to me, Saylor. Let me feel you."

She rolled onto her back and started to get up. "Lie back down. I'll get it," I told her. Her eyes followed my every movement as I pulled on my jeans, walked over to the door, and wheeled the cart of food into the room.

I handed her a folded note. "I think this is for you."

Saylor read it and laughed. "My mom says thanks for knowing roast chicken is her favorite. She thinks I ordered it, but imagine how impressed she'd be to know you did."

Instead of allowing her to get dressed, I held out my hand and led her to the small table by the room's window. "Please sit," I said before unfastening my jeans and letting them fall to the floor. I moved the one other chair next to hers and then set the two domed plates of food on the table.

"May I?" I asked, holding the bottle of wine. When Saylor nodded, I poured two glasses.

"This looks fabulous," she said when I removed the domes and sat next to her. "Thank you, Monk."

Saylor leaned over and kissed the center of my Aztec sun tattoo. "My brother has the same ink."

"He does." I sipped the wine, watching as she brought each morsel of food to her mouth, savoring the flavors.

"I can't take another bite," she groaned after only eating half of the food in front of her. "Would you like more?" she asked, eyeing my empty plate.

Rather than answer, I switched the plates and continued eating.

She leaned back in the chair and closed her eyes.

"Come," I said, holding my hand out to her. "You need to sleep."

"Monk, I can go to my room."

I put my fingertips on her lips. "Sleep with me."

I waited until Saylor's breathing evened out before I let myself close my eyes. I tightened my hold so her body was as close to mine as possible.

I couldn't remember the last time I'd fallen asleep with a woman in my bed, and I didn't bother trying to recall it. No woman I'd slept with came close to comparing with Saylor. Being with her was so easy that sometimes I felt as though she could read my mind.

When my thoughts drifted to her ex, I pushed them away. How a man could strike any woman was unfathomable to me, but to hit Saylor? It was incomprehensible. Her spirit was so pure, flawless like her skin. I'd seen enough of her to know that the way she was with me was the way she was with everyone.

Saylor didn't judge. She accepted. She smiled easily, was very intelligent, and was physically exquisite.

I pushed thoughts of our lovemaking away too. If I didn't, I'd never let her sleep, and we both needed to.

The events of the last few days plagued me. At the end of every mission, the team held a hotwash. The immediate after-action discussions and evaluations every member of the team participated in allowed me to let go of everything that had happened over the course of the op, whether it had been a matter of days or months. My guess was that many of the other partners felt the same way I did. However, with Razor being shot and almost dying, the hotwash hadn't happened.

On this particular mission, the op involved rescuing Ava from the kidnappers that had knocked me out at the fishing cabin, and then assassinating the ringleader.

While Ava had been successfully extracted, along with the three other girls who were being held, Makar Petrov, the assassination target, had gotten away. That meant the threat against Ava hadn't been neutralized; it had been fueled.

Sometime in the next few days, I anticipated a meeting being called during which the team would reconvene to take Petrov down.

With that thought, I let my eyes drift closed.

When the sun came up, I woke Saylor with my body.

"Am I dreaming?" she asked between sweet mewls of pleasure.

I took her softly, knowing she'd be sore from the night before. She accepted it and let my body love hers.

I held her afterwards, and she drifted back to sleep. When I heard room service knock, I eased her off me, pulled on my jeans, and padded to the door.

When I wheeled the cart next to where she lay, Saylor stretched her arms over her head. "Breakfast in bed? I like it."

"You'll want to get back to the hospital. This will make it easier."

"You're very considerate, Monk."

I smiled and handed her a fork.

"What?" she asked.

"I've been accused of being pragmatic more than considerate."

Saylor took a bite of fruit. "You're both."

5

"They're moving you to a regular room, bro," I said, thrilled to find Razor sitting up and looking more like himself. "The doc said you're a damn superhero."

"I've been telling you that since we were kids."

I slugged him, then sat in the chair by his bed. "How's Ava?"

"Fragile."

"Understandably."

"How much do you know about what went down?"

"More than you'd want me to."

"Monk decided now would be a good time to start talking?"

I laughed. "No. Doc's wife, Merrigan, told me some of it. How badass is she, by the way?"

"Ava's father remains a threat."

"What can I do?"

Razor shrugged. "When this is all over, I'm going to ask her to marry me."

"Don't wait, Raze."

"No?"

"You, of all people, should know just how precious life is. Ask her today. Hell, marry her today if she'll have you." I winked.

"Hey, how's Mom doin'?"

"Fine. Didn't you see her a half hour ago?"

"Yeah, but you know how she is."

"She's been a trooper. I have to admit, I was a little surprised."

"She likes Ava, right?"

My eyes filled with tears.

"What?"

"She asked her to be here with us when they took you off life support."

"Wow."

"I know."

"Just to confirm, that means she likes her. Right?"

I slugged him a second time. "You're such a dork. How'd you ever become a spook?"

"Why do people keep saying that to me? And, by the way, we refer to ourselves as agents or officers, not spooks."

"I love you, Razor. Don't ever get shot again."

"I love you too, Saylor." He winced when he tried to sit up straighter.

"Take it easy, Superman."

"Listen, there's something I need you to do for me, kind of along the lines of what we were talking about a minute ago."

"Name it."

"I don't know yet when I'm going to get out of here, but when I do, I know Doc will send the plane, if it isn't here already."

"What does this have to do with me?"

"I'm going to propose."

"On the plane? Ew."

"You haven't been on this plane."

He explained the layout of it and what he wanted me to do.

"Okay, you convinced me. I'll do it. What about a ring?"

"Mom already had that covered."

"How…you know, never mind. The woman never ceases to amaze me."

When I stood to leave, my brother grabbed my wrist. "She said you and Monk—"

I sat back down. "Listen, Raze, I've been where you are, although I'll be the first to admit your choice of a future spouse is way better than mine was. Anyway, my point is, I'm not looking to get into another relationship. Monk is hot as all get-out, and he's a nice enough guy, but that's it for me."

"Mom said you didn't come home last night."

I laughed. "Is that the way she put it? Home? We stayed in a hotel."

He nodded.

"She's a hoot."

"Listen to me, Saylor, Monk is—"

I stood and put my hand on my hip. "Did you not hear a word I said?"

"I did, but—"

"Look, I'll say it again. It doesn't matter what Monk is or isn't. It matters what I am. I have two little girls to raise, neither of which remember their father, thank God. They are my priority. Monk was there last night, and it happened to work for both of us. That's it."

Razor didn't look convinced.

"I know the life you live, my brother. You may be able to take some time off now since you almost died and all, but I've seen exactly how often you come and go. I'm not interested in a relationship with Monk, but even if I were, that alone would be enough for me to rethink it."

I leaned over and kissed his forehead. "I'm the big sister. I worry about you, not the other way around."

When I walked out of Razor's room, Monk was standing in the hallway.

"How long have you been here?"

"Long enough."

"Look, I—"

Monk swept past me, went into Razor's room, and closed the door behind him.

He wasn't upset, right? He just didn't feel like listening to my unnecessary explanation. We were both on the same page. Weren't we? Of course we were.

"You're talking to yourself," said a nurse walking by.

"Yeah, I do that."

"Doesn't everybody?"

I left the ICU in search of my mother. If I was going to do the stuff Razor asked me to, I needed to go shopping.

—Monk—

"Hey, man. My sister was just here," said Razor.

"I saw her."

"Right. Look, the reason I asked you to come in was because I want to thank you for saving Avarie's life."

Seconds before Razor was shot, I'd been able to shoot the gun Petrov had leveled at Ava out of the man's hand. It bought us enough time for Razor to shelter her with his own body.

"I didn't know who he was at the time, and I didn't have the order to kill him."

"I know that, and while I wish the bastard was dead, I am not questioning your actions. You did the exact right thing, and because of it, Ava is alive and so am I."

"Who shot you?"

Razor shook his head. "I have an idea, but Gunner thinks I'm wrong."

"The Russian?"

"Yep. The fact that she disappeared seems proof enough to me."

"Unless somebody took her."

"Do me a favor, and don't repeat those words to Gunner."

"What else do you need from me?"

"I'll leave the details to Doc, but we're going after Petrov with all the firepower we can."

"Copy that," I said, standing.

"Before you leave, I want to talk to you about my sister."

"I know everything there is to know."

"Her ex, he hurt her bad."

"He's in prison."

"I know he is, but that isn't my point. What I'm trying to say is, she's built a brick wall around herself."

"You heard her. She isn't looking for a relationship. Neither am I."

"Okay. As long as you're on the same page."

I walked out of the ICU, relieved Saylor wasn't waiting for me. I hadn't expected her to be, but I never knew when it came to women. I was also relieved to know she was exactly who I thought she was. No nonsense. No bullshit. Great sex. A little comfort given between two people who were hurting. End of story.

I checked in with Doc. When he said I wasn't needed for anything presently, I took a walk.

The hospital was in the kind of neighborhood I liked: not quite gentrified, but on its way. I stopped in a bookstore that had a used-book section and picked up a couple of mysteries I'd been wanting to read.

A few doors down, I saw a coffee shop with tables out front. I set the two books on a table and went inside to order.

"Hi," someone said.

I turned around and saw Saylor seated by the window with her mother. "Hi, Saylor. Sally." I took the woman's outstretched hand.

"Thank you for dinner last night, Monk."

I was about to turn around to order when Sally stood and walked around me. "Excuse me," she said, pointing to the restrooms.

"Nice seein' you," I said to Saylor.

"Wait, Monk. Do you have time to sit for a minute?"

"Sure." I sat in the chair her mother had just vacated.

"I really enjoyed the time we spent together last night. I want you to know that."

"Me too."

"It's just that…my life…your life."

I leaned forward and rested my arms on the table. "Let me tell you what I think, since I already heard what you think."

"Okay." She sat back in her chair and folded her arms.

"From the first moment I saw you, I wanted you. That hasn't changed. I have no idea what tomorrow will bring. I never do. As you told your brother, you know exactly how our lives work. I'll tell you this, though; if you and I are in the same place at the same time and there's a chance I can feel your naked body next to mine, I'll take it."

"*Jesus,*" she muttered, making me smile more. "What woman could resist that?"

I stood and leaned over her, my mouth near her ear. "I don't care what any other woman would or wouldn't do."

I put my fingers on her cheek, turned her head, and kissed her. It wasn't a chaste kiss. I didn't waste time with shit like that. I loved the way Saylor's tongue played with the silver ball on the tip of mine.

I broke the kiss when I heard Sally clear her throat. "I'll see you later."

"Okay," Saylor murmured.

"Bye, Monk," said Sally.

"Bye, Sally."

I walked out of the coffee shop, picked the books up I'd left on the table, and kept walking.

6

—Saylor—

My mother fanned her face. "Wow."

"Stop it."

"Not a chance. Tell me what he said."

"You've got to be kidding."

"Saylor, there hasn't been a time in your life when you didn't tell me everything, whether I wanted to hear it or not. Don't stop now."

"He said that if he and I are in the same place at the same time and there's a chance he can feel my naked body next to his, he'd take it."

"What did you say?"

"I asked what woman could resist that."

"And." My mother motioned with her hand for me to continue.

"He told me he didn't care what other women thought."

She sat back in her chair.

"Go ahead, say whatever it is."

"I'd say, beloved daughter of mine, that you have finally met your match."

I rolled my eyes. "It's just sex, Mom."

"You keep telling yourself that."

When Razor called the next morning to say that he was being discharged that afternoon and that Doc was making arrangements for me to get on the plane, I rolled over and kissed Monk's Aztec sun tattoo.

"I gotta go decorate a plane."

He reached up, cupped my cheek with his big hand, and brought his lips to mine.

"God, you can kiss," I said when he let go.

"So can you."

"My mom and I are leaving today."

"I heard."

"Noon flight."

"I'll see you later, Saylor."

I smiled. "Yeah, see you later, Monk."

I grabbed my clothes and walked into the bathroom, dressed, and left without saying another word.

I let myself into the room next door and found my mother dressed and sipping a cup of coffee. "Ready?" she asked.

"I need to shower," I muttered, grabbing clean clothes and slipping into the bathroom. "And before I come back out, I want you to wipe that smug look off your face."

Twenty minutes later, my mother still looked just as pleased with herself. I laughed.

"Let's go. I need coffee, seeing as you didn't order any for me."

"What, no breakfast in bed today?"

"I'm not telling you anything ever again."

"It looks beautiful, Saylor," my mother said later when we'd finished decorating the stateroom on K19's plane.

We'd hung strands of twinkle lights in rows from the ceiling and strewn red rose petals on the bed—all per my brother's request. The only thing left to do was put the bottle of champagne in a bucket of ice, and that I'd ask Alegria to do when she knew Razor and Ava were on their way.

"We need to go, or we're going to miss our flight," I said to my mom, pulling her out of the stateroom.

"Shame," she said as we walked up the aisle. "I always wanted to fly on a private plane."

"You just did a few days ago."

"That was a little one, and nowhere near as nice as this one."

"I'll ask Razor to arrange a flight for your birthday."

"You're a big chicken," my mother mumbled.

"I am not."

"Are too."

"Seeing as we didn't have time to eat, I need sustenance before our flight. Hurry up."

The whole way down the stairs, onto the tarmac, and into the main terminal of the airport, my mother clucked like a chicken.

—Monk—

I got up when I heard the hotel room door close, stretched my arms above my head, and rolled my shoulders. My body screamed at me to get to the gym, which I'd be able to do once we were back in Yachats.

I anticipated Doc would call the hotwash meeting soon after our arrival, and then I'd find out where this nomadic life would take me next.

The only thing I knew for certain was that Petrov would be our number one target. That much was a given. Ava's life would remain in danger until we were able to find the man and take him down.

Saylor, though. *Damn.* There wasn't a single thing I didn't like about the woman, including her not wanting a relationship. It wasn't that I didn't want one either; it was more that a relationship wouldn't fit into my life. Just like it didn't fit into hers.

However, she had invaded my thoughts for most of the morning.

When I got back to Yachats, she'd be there. It's where she lived. Where my job with K19 would take me next made me wonder how long would it be before I saw Saylor again? Taking down Petrov was a mission that would involve putting my life in danger many times over. If I died, would my last thoughts be of her?

I checked my phone and saw there was a message from Doc saying that I was to pick up one of four SUVs we'd be using to escort Razor from the hospital to the airfield. The number of vehicles and personnel in them wasn't for Razor's protection as much as for his peace of mind. As one of the four founding partners, the man could call in as much K19 firepower as he wanted, and when it came to keeping Ava safe, I was surprised Razor hadn't demanded tanks along with closed airspace.

I got in the shower, turned the temperature all the way to hot, and stood under the scalding, cascading water. I eased the temp back once I felt the tension in my shoulders loosen and the fog clearing from my head. The job I did, required that I be one hundred percent focused, one hundred percent in the game. There was no room for any clouds of judgment.

There'd been a time in my life when I considered taking up the sport of bull riding. It took the same mindset. If a rider wasn't all in, every thought, every breath focused on staying on the back of that bull, he faced certain death.

I dressed, repacked my small bag, and was ready to head out, but turned around and took one more look at the bed I'd shared with Saylor last night and the one before. I closed my eyes, breathing in the scent of her and of our lovemaking. Both lingered in my memory, if not in the air.

I pulled the SUV up to the front of the hospital just as Razor and Ava came out the door. I got out and approached the two when Razor motioned me over.

"Stay close, just in case," he muttered as he climbed into the second row of seats, behind Ava. The man had survived a gunshot wound that penetrated both lungs, put him on life support, and yet he was leaving the hospital four days later. I would've gladly carried him out if he would have needed it. Razor Sharp was a goddamn rock star, though. It was an honor to get to work with him as often as I did.

As I'd expected, Razor climbed the stairs onto the K19 plane unassisted. I wished I could've seen how Saylor had decorated the aft stateroom, but it wasn't for my eyes; it was for Ava's. Judging by the way she gasped when Razor opened the door, it must've been beautiful.

When I turned around to take a seat, Onyx was studying me. "Heard you been keepin' company with Razor's sister."

The pilot, with his quiff haircut and signature Randolph aviator sunglasses, had become one of my closest friends. We'd met when we served together in the Marine Corps. He had flown F/A-18 Hornets, and like me, didn't feel the need to fill a silent void with conversation.

"You got it bad, son," Onyx said when I sat in one of the plane's captain's chairs and he caught me smiling.

He lingered a few seconds before walking toward the cockpit, chuckling as he went.

Maybe he was right and I did have it bad; that didn't mean I wouldn't be over it soon.

7

"We just landed," I told my best friend, Poppy, who the girls were staying with. "I'll come straight there to get them."

"I'll bring them to the house."

"You don't have to do that. I don't want to put you out more than I already have." I laughed. "Like I always do."

"You know I love these girls more than I love you. You aren't putting me out."

I laughed again.

"Plus, if I don't bring them to you, you'll be in a hurry to get home, and we have a lot to talk about, girlfriend."

"We do? What have you heard?"

"Uh, I have a life too, you know?"

"Jeez. Sorry. It is always about me, isn't it?"

"No, it never is, but I do have something to tell you."

"How are the girls?" my mother asked when I ended the call.

I shook my head. "The girls? Why would I ask about the girls?" What was wrong with me? However, if there were anything wrong with either Sierra or Savannah, Poppy would've said so. Still, I should've asked.

I pulled into the driveway and carried my mom's suitcase into her side of the duplex first, amid protests that she was perfectly capable of doing it herself.

I leaned forward and kissed her cheek. "I'm sure the girls will be over to see their Ya-Ya very soon."

She put her palm on my cheek. "Are you okay?"

"Why? Don't I seem okay?"

"You're distracted."

"I'm fine. See ya later, Mom."

I walked out. I wanted to see my girls, and I didn't want to talk about Monk, as I was sure my mother did.

"Where are my doodlebugs?" I shouted, walking in the back door.

"Mama! Mama! Mama!" They both came running, almost tackling me to the ground.

"You look so big. Did you grow another inch while I was gone?"

"Maybe," said Savannah, to which Sierra rolled her eyes.

"Did you behave yourselves?"

"We painted Aunt Poppy's spare bedroom for her," answered Savannah.

My eyes opened wide, and I looked over at Poppy. "You did?"

"She asked us to," said Sierra with one hand on her hip.

"That's certainly good to hear."

"See ya, Mama," said Savannah, running back to her bedroom with Sierra on her heels.

I hugged Poppy. "Hi. So, redecorating?"

"We were bored."

"How does it look?"

"About as good as you'd expect it to."

I cringed. "Coffee?"

"Absolutely. Why is coffee so much better when someone else makes it?"

"What's going on, Pop?"

"There's a guy."

I spun around, spilling coffee grounds on the kitchen counter. *"Who?"* In our small town of Yachats, there weren't many single guys left.

"He's from Portland. Nothing much has happened yet, but I like him."

It sounded similar to Monk and me, only something had happened between us.

Poppy took the bag of coffee and the scoop out of my hand.

"Sit. I'll make it."

"I can do it."

"Right. Go sit down and tell me whatever it is that's on your mind."

"There's a guy," I repeated Poppy's words.

"No shit? Who?"

"He works with my brother."

"I see."

"His name is Monk. That isn't his name, but that's what everyone calls him." It occurred to me that I'd spent two nights with the guy, had several rounds of amazing sex, and I had no idea what his real first name was. I shook my head.

"What was that all about?"

Poppy and I had been friends since we were younger than my two girls; there wasn't much I could hide from her.

"Just that I don't know his name. Enough of that. Tell me about your guy."

"We met at Speed, actually."

The local coffee shop. I should have stopped there to get coffee since neither of us seemed capable of actually brewing a pot.

"We went out later, for dinner, and then he had to go back to Portland."

"Did he say when he'd be back?"

Poppy shook her head. "I really like him, though."

"What do you like about him?"

"He's sexy as fuck—" Poppy looked over her shoulder to make sure neither of the girls was within hearing distance. "Anyway, you get what I'm saying. Tell me about Monk."

He was sexy as fuck too, but otherwise, where did I begin? The guy was unlike any other I'd ever met.

"My mom said she thinks I've met my match."

"Stubborn smart-ass who has sworn off relationships for the rest of his life?"

"Essentially."

"If that's the case, why did you say there's a guy."

"I said 'there's.' It could mean there was a guy."

"If he were a was, you wouldn't have brought it up."

"I don't know. I mean, I don't know if I'll ever see him again. I'll see him, of course; Razor works out of his house here almost exclusively now. But that doesn't mean I'll see him."

"Let me get this straight. You aren't sure you're going to see him." Poppy rolled her eyes like I had earlier.

"Shut up."

"Mama, that's a bad word! You owe me a dollar," shouted Sierra from the bedroom.

"She heard shut up and not fuck?" whispered Poppy.

"Do you want to go out for coffee?" I asked, looking at the coffee pot that I hadn't turned on yet.

"A cocktail sounds better at this point."

"Agreed."

We took the trail that ran along the ocean. It began ten miles north of my house and went all the way through the downtown district and another ten miles south. It was one of my favorite things about living right on the coast. I wouldn't have been able to afford it if my brother hadn't bought the duplex for our mom and me. I sure as hell never got a penny of child support from my ex, especially given he was in prison.

"Don't get too far ahead," I called out to the girls. Poppy and I took our time. "Stop before you round the bend." That was our agreement; if they couldn't make eye contact with me, they needed to come back.

"Razor almost died," I blurted. "He was on life support."

Poppy stopped walking. "I wondered why you didn't call for a couple of days. I knew something was up."

"He was shot rescuing Ava."

"Wow."

Poppy knew better than to ask more questions. Most of the time, I couldn't say a word about whatever my brother was involved in—not that I ever knew as much as I did this time. If he knew I'd told Poppy about his health scare, he probably wouldn't like it, but I needed to share with someone who hadn't been there and experienced the same fear I had.

"Are you okay?" she asked.

"I don't know, to be honest. I'm not sure it's really hit me yet."

Poppy nodded and we kept walking.

"He asked Ava to marry him."

"Would you stop doing that!"

"What?"

"Saying these things that I really should be sitting down to hear. Anything else? *You* aren't married, are you?"

"Don't be ridiculous."

However, the idea that Razor would ever get married had previously been as unimaginable as me doing it again.

Four hours later, Poppy had gone home. I couldn't bring myself to leave the perch from where I could see when Razor's caravan pulled in.

I was turning into as much of a busybody as my neighbor had been when the girls and I still lived with their dad.

Just as I stood to go into the bedroom, I saw an SUV pull up. Unfortunately, it went into the garage before I could see who was in it. "You're such an idiot," I mumbled, going down the hall to make sure the girls hadn't decided to paint their bedroom like they had Poppy's.

"Hey, Mama," said Sierra, looking up from her coloring book.

"I sure missed you two."

"We missed you too, Mama," said Savannah, looking up from hers.

"Do you want to go next door and see Ya-Ya?"

"We saw her before we went into town."

"I know, but you can't see too much of Ya-Ya, can you?"

"When will Aunt Ava be home?"

"What about Uncle Razor?" I asked.

"Him too."

"Maybe we'll be able to see them tomorrow."

Savannah jumped up. "Are they home?"

"I think so, but Uncle Razor was in the hospital for a few days, and I'm sure he's very tired."

"Was Aunt Ava in the hospital too?"

"Sort of. She spent a lot of time with Uncle Razor while he was there."

Both girls looked crestfallen enough that I thought about calling to see if I could bring them over. But not knowing if Monk had arrived with them stopped me. I didn't want him to think I used the girls as an excuse to come see him.

I shook my head. Wasn't this just as bad? I was avoiding going to see my beloved brother, who had almost died, because I was too worried about what Monk thought. Not to mention I wanted to know whether Ava had said yes when he proposed.

"Up for some company, or are you too wiped out?" I asked when Razor answered his phone. "Savannah and Sierra are anxious to see you."

"Don't lie, Saylor," he said, laughing. "They want to see Ava more than they want to see me."

"You're right. Sorry, bro."

"That's okay. I'd rather see Avarie over anyone else too."

"Thanks a bunch, Raze."

"Whatever. Come over here."

—Monk—

I offered to find another place to stay, but Razor told me he wanted me at the house.

"Until the risk has been neutralized, I want Ava protected at all times."

"Roger that," I responded before going downstairs. I threw my bag on the office's pullout sofa, where I'd slept before we went to Washington.

I looked up and saw Razor standing in the doorway. "First of all," he said, "you can't sleep in here. There's a bedroom upstairs at the end of the hall. Secondly, my sister is on her way over with my nieces."

I picked up my bag. "Anything else?"

"We have a new system being delivered soon." Razor motioned to the equipment in the office.

"Yeah?"

"Something Burns has been working on."

"Anything you need me to do?"

"Touch base with him and ask."

"Roger that." Burns Butler, Doc Butler's father, was a technological wizard. I couldn't wait to see what the man had come up with this time.

I reached the top of the stairs at the same time there was a knock on the front door. I walked over and opened it when I saw it was Saylor.

"Where's Aunt Ava?" her two girls shrieked as they ran past me.

"Hi," said Saylor. "They couldn't wait."

"Hi." I stepped aside so she could come in.

"Going somewhere?" she asked, looking down at the bag I was carrying.

"Bedroom down the hall."

"Okay, well, nice to see you."

Saylor walked by, not making eye contact.

"See you later, Saylor." She didn't turn around, but from where I stood, I could see the flush that pinkened her cheeks.

I carried my bag down the hall, tossed it into the bedroom, and walked back out and into the kitchen.

"Is that Monk?" I heard Ava ask, looking up from where she braided Sierra's hair like she'd done to Savannah's.

"What would you like, Ava?"

"Whatever you're making. I'm starving. If you don't mind, that is. I know you're not here to cook for us."

I looked through the contents of the refrigerator and then the pantry. There wasn't a lot of fresh food in the house, but I could probably whip something together without it. I pulled out a box of linguine, a few cans of clams, and a bottle of white wine. There was minced garlic in the refrigerator and lemon juice.

"Razor wasn't kidding when he said you were a chef."

When I turned around, Saylor was sitting at the kitchen bar.

"I enjoy cooking."

"It looks that way. Do you need anything? My house is two doors down."

I knew where it was. In fact, I knew a lot more about Saylor Sharp-Davis than either she or her brother would probably like.

"I can make do."

She shrugged and walked back over to where Ava sat with the two girls.

I heard one of them ask if they could have a sleepover with Ava, but Saylor quickly shot the idea down. "Maybe another time when Uncle Razor is feeling better."

I didn't hear either girl argue. I liked that.

"Do you have any fresh herbs?" I asked from the kitchen doorway, suddenly wishing I could take her in my arms and kiss her.

"I have an herb garden."

I'd known before I asked. Given I was here as part of Ava's detail, it was my job to be situationally aware.

"What kind of herbs do you need?"

"Mind if I take a look at your garden for myself?"

"Will you be okay with the girls for a few minutes?" I heard Saylor ask Ava. I didn't catch the answer, but she stood and walked over to me. "I'll go with you. I live in that—"

I pulled the front door closed behind us, grabbed her around the waist, and pushed her up against the outside wall. I brought my hand to her neck and held her in place, capturing her mouth with mine.

Saylor put her arms around my neck and kissed me back. I leaned my body into hers as our tongues tangled. Just kissing her made me hard. Feeling her breasts against my chest made it painful.

I ended the kiss, backed away, and took her hand, leading her off the porch.

"Can I come in?" I asked when she muttered something about being right back (seems like something is missing after we arrived at her house.

"Uh…sure."

I followed her into the kitchen where she opened a drawer and handed me a pair of heavy-duty kitchen shears.

"I use these in the garden," she said.

I took the scissors from her hand and set them on the kitchen counter. I rested my ass against it and pulled Saylor's body flush with mine. Reaching down, I pulled my shirt up and then hers, not over her head, but enough that I could feel her bare skin next to mine. With both hands on her cheeks, I kissed her deeper than before.

"I could do this for hours."

Saylor pulled away, her skin flushed, breathing accelerated, and her pupils dilated. "We should get back."

I picked up the scissors and followed her out of the house and into the garden.

"Would you mind?" I asked, pointing to the lettuce and spinach.

"Not at all."

She went back inside while I snipped the greens, and came out with a basket made of wood and mesh. She set it on the ground near me. "I have a cucumber too, and red and yellow grape tomatoes."

"And snap peas," I added, pulling two from the vine and eating the first in one bite. "So sweet. Taste." I brought the one still in my hand to her mouth. When she took it, she nipped my fingers. I laughed.

"I'm on security detail," I said on the walk back to her brother's place. "I'll be here for a while."

Saylor looked out at the ocean but didn't respond.

"I want your body next to mine, Saylor."

She looked me in the eye. "The girls…their lives…I know they don't remember, but I need to protect them."

"I'm sorry if I overstepped."

"We'll talk, but some other time." She dropped my hand, ran up the porch steps, and into the house.

"Sorry to cut our visit short, but we have lots to do, girls. I'm sure Uncle Razor and Aunt Ava are getting hungry. We don't want to keep them from having dinner, right?"

From the kitchen, I could see the little girls hug Ava and blow kisses to their uncle. I went back to the sink to wash the vegetables I'd gotten from Saylor's garden.

"Bye, Mr. Monk," I heard a small voice say from the doorway.

I dried my hands, walked over, and bent down. "Goodbye, Miss Savannah. I hope to see you again soon."

"Bye," said Sierra, holding onto Saylor with one hand while she waved at me with the other.

"Bye, Miss Sierra."

I stood and looked into their mother's eyes. "I'll see you soon, Saylor."

"Bye, Monk."

8

"Ava is beginning to think you don't like her," said Razor, who showed up at my garden gate several days later, scaring the crap out of me.

"That's silly."

"She wants Sierra and Savannah to be flower girls."

"What does that have to do with me?"

Razor crouched down next to where I was pulling weeds and rested his hand on my arm. "Saylor, look at me."

I tossed the garden tool on the ground, wiped my hands on my shorts, and sat on my butt in the grass. "What?"

"We've been home two weeks, and we've hardly seen you."

"What the eff, Raze? I've gone months without seeing you."

"I'm not talking about me. I'm talking about Ava."

"It's awkward, okay? I'm sorry if I've hurt Ava's feelings, but I'd rather not run into Monk."

"Why not?"

I got back on my knees and continued my assault on the plants that didn't belong in my garden.

"It isn't like you to let a man keep you away from your family."

I stood and threw the trowel on the ground. "Don't pull that shit with me, Tabon. I don't want to see him, and I don't fucking care what you think. How dare you throw anything about Cliff in my face?"

Razor stood too. "This isn't about Cliff."

"Isn't it? If I remember right, you said almost those exact same words to me a few months after I started dating him."

"This is different. Monk isn't keeping you from us. You're keeping yourself away because you don't want to see him."

I went into the house, but he followed.

"I'll reassign him if that's what it takes."

"I just need a little time. Things were moving too fast, getting too serious."

My brother raised a brow.

"Okay, so maybe it wasn't getting too serious, but he wanted more from me than I could give."

"Like I said, I'll reassign him. Done deal." He opened the door to leave.

"Don't do that. It isn't fair to him."

"No, it'll be easier if he just works out of another office."

"Razor, please don't do that."

"Right," he said, looking at the vase on the kitchen bar. "Nice flowers."

They'd come the week after everyone got back from Washington, which was also a week since I'd seen Monk. Even though they came from a florist, they looked more like he'd gone out and picked a bouquet of wildflowers himself.

"I'll be over later," I called after him.

"Come for dinner."

"Don't push it, Raze."

He laughed and walked over to the trail.

An hour later, my mother, the girls, and I walked into my brother's house when Ava opened the door.

"Where's Razor?" I asked later when I still hadn't seen him.

"He and Monk are downstairs. A truckload of new equipment arrived, and they've been setting it all up. I guess it's taken over most of the basement."

The girls had their noses buried in bridal magazines and didn't seem to be paying attention, so I took the opportunity to apologize to Ava.

"One, you're forgiven, and two, it wasn't me who was upset; it was your brother."

"That jerk."

"Yeah, that's what I said when he told me what he said to you. Don't get me wrong, I love your company, but it isn't like I expect you to be over here all the time. You have a life of your own."

"Thank you," I huffed, ready to go downstairs and slug my brother.

Instead, when I looked over, he and Monk were coming up the stairs.

"How's flower-girl dress-buying going?" Razor asked, walking over and kissing Ava's forehead.

"They want every one they see," I answered. "Ava, you really just need to choose for them, or they'll drive you mad."

"We don't drive yet," said Savannah, looking over her shoulder at me and sticking a playful tongue out.

"What do you think, Mr. Monk," said Sierra, walking over to him with magazine in hand. He crouched down like he had when he said goodbye to Savannah a few days ago.

"You would look beautiful in any of these," he said, pointing at something on the page. "But I think this one would look the very best."

"That's my favorite too," Sierra said, flouncing back over to her sister.

"Let me see which one," Savannah demanded. "That was my favorite," she said when Sierra pointed. "I picked that one first."

"You did not."

"Yes, I did."

"Girls," I scolded. "That's enough."

"Sorry, Mama," they both said, hanging their heads. They took the magazine over to Ava.

"You should pick," said Sierra.

"Show me the one Mr. Monk likes best."

Ava clapped her hands when they showed her. "That was my favorite too. We all liked the same one." She winked at me.

"Avarie," said Razor. "We need to leave now if we're going to meet your sister."

"That's right," she said, jumping up. "Sorry we have to leave so abruptly." She kissed my cheek and then each of the girls. "I'll see you tomorrow so the dressmaker can get your measurements, right?"

Both Savannah and Sierra nodded.

"I'm in a rush too," said Sally. "I was supposed to be at Mahjong fifteen minutes ago."

"We'll drop you off," Razor offered, ushering our mother into the car.

"Thank you," I said to Monk after everyone else drove off. "You were very sweet with them."

"They're nice girls." Monk stood next to me and brushed his fingertips against mine. "I've missed seeing you."

"I know. I'm sorry. I just—"

"No apology is necessary."

"Thank you for the flowers."

"They reminded me of you."

I felt fourteen again, having an awkward conversation with my first boyfriend.

"Mama," said Savannah, tugging on my arm.

"What is it, doodlebug?" I asked, bending down.

"Invite Mr. Monk over for dinner."

"Oh, I'm sure he's too busy, but it's sweet of you to think of it."

"I have the night off."

"Please," my daughter begged.

"What should we make for Mr. Monk?" I asked. "Do you know what he likes to eat?"

Savannah looked up at him. "What's your favorite food?"

"Hmm," he said, scratching his beard that had grown much longer since I last saw him. "I'd have to say pizza."

"Pizza? That's my favorite."

"No, it isn't," said Sierra, stalking over to them. "My favorite is pizza. Yours is Chinese."

"No, it isn't."

"Yes—"

"Girls," I warned with a stern look.

"My mama makes the best pizza in the world," Sierra told Monk.

"I'm sure whatever she makes is the best in the world." He turned to me. "I can help."

"No helping necessary," I said. "You'll be our guest. How's six? The girls are in bed by eight."

"Why don't I just walk with you now?"

—Monk—

"We could order out," I suggested as we walked two houses over.

"I really do make good pizza."

"You were blindsided."

"I know how to say no, Monk."

I smiled. "Based on how well-behaved your girls are, you must be very good at it."

Saylor smiled too. "Thank you. I think."

"It was a compliment."

"It isn't easy, I can tell you that. Yachats is a very small place, and there aren't many divorced families in it. Sometimes, I think having only one parent is harder on them than they'd ever admit to me."

I put my hand on her shoulder, unable to resist touching her. "You're a good mom."

"I'm sorry I haven't been around much."

"Don't," I said, stopping to turn her body toward me. "I told you before not to apologize. I like you, Saylor, and I like your girls. I'd consider it an honor to get to know all three of you better."

"I can't promise anything."

"Neither can I."

Sierra and Savannah had been right about how good their mother's pizza was. She made the dough and the sauce from scratch and then let each of them pick their toppings, most of which were fresh vegetables.

When we finished dinner, Saylor refused to let me help clean up, which left me available to be the third player in Pigmania.

"You have to say it," pressed Savannah when I rolled all my pigs upside down. "Listen, it goes like this. '*Soooooie.*' Now you try it."

Every time I tried, I laughed too hard to get it out. I looked into the kitchen, and Saylor was laughing as hard as I was.

"Oh…my…gosh," said Sierra, hand on hip as she did so often. "He can't say it, Savannah; just give him a pass."

"That means it's the end of the game and I won," said Savannah.

"She cheats," said Sierra as she put the game away.

"Bath time, girls," Saylor said from the kitchen.

"Yes, Mama," they answered in unison before heading down the hallway.

"They would do well in the south."

"What do you mean?" Saylor asked, coming to sit on the sofa next to me.

"Their manners."

"Are you from the south, Monk?"

"Yes, ma'am," I said, exaggerating the accent I'd lost years ago.

"I was thinking the other day, I don't even know your first name."

"Rhys, but spelled differently than the peanut butter cup. I've been called Monk since I was a kid, though."

"I guess you didn't talk much then either."

"I didn't." I found myself wanting to tell Saylor about my sister and how her murder had resulted in my difficulty communicating, but it was too soon for a conversation like that. "Thank you for dinner," I said instead.

"Thank you for joining us."

I turned so I was facing her. "Tell me how I can spend time with you."

"Monk, I…"

"Ground rules?"

"Are you serious?"

"Yes. Set some."

"Okay, but remember, you asked for this."

"I did."

"No sleepovers. That's a big one. No PDA of any kind."

"Hand-holding?"

"It depends on the circumstance."

"Roger that."

Saylor chuckled. "The girls are my number one priority, and whatever they need comes first."

"What else?"

"That's a lot, Monk. The only thing we've really done is…uh…have sleepovers."

I stroked my finger down the side of her face. I wanted to do so much more, but I'd respect the boundaries she'd put in place.

"I like this," she said, stroking my beard. She rested her palm against my cheek. "This isn't going to be easy. I so want to kiss you right now."

I wanted so much more—to pick her up, carry her into the bedroom, strip off her clothes, and keep her there for a month. Instead, I took her hand in mine and brought the palm to my lips. "I should go."

"Yes. Okay."

She stood when I did.

"Please say good night to the girls and thank them for me."

"I will."

9

"What are you doing?"

"Hi, Saylor. How are you?"

"Hi, Poppy. Sorry. Are you busy?"

"I was just about to put a thing of popcorn in the microwave. Does that constitute 'busy'?"

"Can you come over?"

"Be there in five."

I went in to check on the girls for the fourth time. They were both still asleep. Not that I expected them to wake up.

I heard the kitchen door open and flew down the hallway. "Thanks for coming over."

"Here. Pop this," my friend said, holding out the package.

"It might wake up the girls."

Poppy ripped the cellophane off, put the bag in the microwave, and set it for three minutes. "A freight train through your living room might wake them up too, but I doubt it. What's going on?"

"The girls invited Monk over for dinner. They asked me first, of course, but he came."

Poppy turned toward me, bent her arm, and rested her head on her hand. "Fascinating. Tell me more," she deadpanned.

"We set ground rules."

"I'm riveted."

"Stop it."

"Saylor, what actually *happened*?"

"He wants to spend time with us."

Poppy grabbed two bowls and the bag of now-popped corn.

"Here, open it."

"There's steam. You have to wait so you don't get burned."

"By that time, it will be cold."

I grabbed the bag, ripped it open, and handed it to her. "Why do I always have to be the one to open it?"

"Because I don't want to get burned." My friend tossed several pieces of popcorn in her mouth. "So, tell me the rest about Monk."

"Don't chew with your mouth open."

"That's it. I'm leaving," she said, not making any move to get up. "What's freaking you out?"

"I don't do the boyfriend thing. You know this."

She sat on the sofa and looked up at the ceiling. "It's time, Saylor. The official cutoff for relationship abstinence after a breakup is five years. You're there."

"I don't know…"

"I'm being serious. You want this and you know it. Plus, if this Monk guy ever even looked at you cross-eyed, your brother would kill him." She ate more popcorn. "Tell me your rules."

"No sleepovers. No PDA."

"That's it?"

"I could set more if you have any suggestions."

"You still get to have sex, though, right?"

I shrugged. "I guess so. If the girls aren't home."

"What's he doing Friday night?"

"Very funny."

"This is me being serious. I'll invite the girls over. We'll repaint the bedroom walls, and you can have a sleepover too."

"He might be busy."

"If he's still busy after you invite him over for sex, dump him. He's a weirdo."

"Are you sure?"

"Yep."

"Thanks, Poppy."

"No problem. You can do something for me too. You can find me one of these hot spy guys of my own."

"What happened to Portland guy?"

"Haven't heard a word from him."

"I'm sorry, Poppy, but to be honest, it would be worse if you got involved with someone who works with my brother."

I knew that firsthand.

The next day, I walked over to Razor's, not to see him or Ava, but to see Monk. As I approached the house, I found him sitting out on the deck. He lifted a hand and waved.

"They aren't here," he said when I came up the steps.

"By they, do you mean my brother and Ava?"

Monk grinned. "Yes."

"Doesn't matter. I'm here to see you."

He leaned forward and put his elbows on his knees. "I like that you're smiling."

I pulled one of the deck chairs closer and sat down. "I'm here to ask you out on a date."

Monk sat up. "I accept."

"What if you have other plans?"

"I'll change them."

"Wow, I didn't even have to offer up sex."

Monk cocked his head.

"It was a joke that doesn't seem that funny anymore."

"Where are the girls now?" he asked.

"Hanging out with Ya-Ya."

"At home?"

I cocked my head like he had. "No, why?"

"Come here." Monk took my hand and pulled me onto his lap. "I need some PDA."

"Me too." I wrapped my arms around his neck.

"When and where is our date?"

"Friday, and uh, my place?"

Monk shook his head. "I'll pick you up at…where will the girls be?"

"At my friend Poppy's house, and she'll probably pick them up around five."

"I'll be there at a minute after." He winked. "Wear something nice."

"We don't have to—"

Monk put his fingertips on my lips. "Yesterday, I asked you to tell me how I could spend more time with you, and I also told you I want to get to know you better."

Was I really ready for this? I kept my heart under lock and key for a damn good reason.

There was so much I liked about Monk, though. The sex was fantastic, but he was also smart and funny and charming. That combination meant I was susceptible to so much more than disappointment. I could fall for him and get my heart broken for the second time in my life. When, not if, that happened, I'd never recover from it.

He cupped my cheek with his palm. "Baby steps, Saylor."

"Are you reading my mind, Monk?"

He tightened his hold on me, and I put my head on his shoulder.

"I know you struggle with wanting to protect your girls. I also know you struggle with doing the same for yourself. It doesn't take a mind reader to know I am pushing you past your comfort zone. The truth is, I am as far out of my own, but each time my head reminds me of that, my heart tells it to shut up."

I turned my head and kissed his neck. "Thank you."

"I'll see you later, Saylor."

"Yes, you will, Monk, but not until Friday."

—*Monk*—

Saylor got off my lap and walked down the steps of the deck to the trail that would lead back to her place.

As much as I missed the warmth of her body close to mine, I couldn't complain about having the opportunity to watch her walk away.

Her long dark hair was up in a ponytail that swished back and forth as she walked, and her legs looked impossibly long in her cutoff shorts. The snugness of her t-shirt gave me a quick reminder of how she'd looked naked in my arms.

I'd been getting ready to go for a run when she walked up, and I was glad I hadn't missed her.

I stood and ran down the steps. "Saylor," I called after her.

She turned and shielded her eyes from the sun.

"Are you a runner?"

"I used to be."

"I was about to go down to the beach."

"To run?"

"Yes."

"Let me change my shoes, and I'll join you."

When Saylor came back out, she'd changed her shorts and shirt too. She threw her leg up on the bench in front of her house and stretched.

"It's been a long time, so don't feel as though you have to wait up for me if I fall behind."

I kept my pace slow and even, and Saylor kept up just fine.

"Can I ask you a question?"

"Of course."

"My brother always says that I can ask but that doesn't mean he'll answer. Thank you for not saying that."

"Ask, and then I have something I want to tell you."

"Uh, okay. Are you sure you don't want to go first?"

I shook my head. "Ask."

"I know that some of the people with K19 are partners, and then others are contractors."

"I fall into the second category."

"Are you working for my brother right now? I mean, is that why you're here in Yachats?"

"Yes. Ava remains in danger, as much as Razor would like to keep that fact from her."

"You disagree."

I shook my head. I didn't agree or disagree.

"What did you want to tell me?"

"When you thanked me for not saying the same thing Razor always says, it reminded me to thank you for not complaining on my usually quiet nature."

Saylor stopped running and put her hands on her knees. "You're welcome." She turned around and looked in the direction from which we'd come. "I usually do sprints back up to the point."

"When you used to be a runner?"

She laughed. "As far as not commenting…I don't see what the big deal is. You talk just as much as everyone else does."

"No. I don't."

"Okay." Her forehead creased, and her eyes scrunched.

"I only talk this much with you."

The crease went away, and her eyes lit up with a smile. "Thank you for saying that."

"Why did you ask if I was a contractor?"

"There's a chance you'll be hired to work somewhere else."

"That is possible."

A little over a week later, I received confirmation that I would, in fact, remain on Ava's detail indefinitely, along with Dutch Miller, a CIA agent I'd worked with back when I was with the company.

"Big meeting at some fishing cabin," Dutch said, tossing his gear on the floor when I opened the door.

Razor had made me aware of the meeting as well as Dutch's impending arrival.

"By the way, I resigned from the agency, effective this morning. So did Striker."

"Does this have anything to do with the mission to take down Petrov?"

Dutch walked over to the windows and looked down at the beach. "It has everything to do with it. I'm also your relief for the afternoon."

Razor had made me aware of that as well. Although he hadn't told me about Dutch's resignation.

"Come with me, and I'll introduce you."

"That kind of detail, huh?" Dutch asked.

"Ava will soon be Razor's wife."

He nodded as though that was enough information for him. "Before we leave the house, Doc Butler asked me to give this to you."

I took the envelope from his hands, carried it to the back bedroom, and then led him down the steps to the beach.

Twenty minutes after leaving Dutch on the beach and climbing back up to the house, I finished reading K19's proposal just as Razor walked in.

"Where are they?" Razor asked when I met him near the stairs.

"The beach. Dutch is with them."

Razor looked out the window. "No one else has arrived yet?"

"Negative. Just Ava and her mother at this point."

"Doc wants to meet with you and Dutch this afternoon."

I held up my phone when it vibrated. "Just got the message."

"It'll be good to have you as an official part of the K19 team."

"I haven't accepted yet."

"No?" Razor laughed. "What are your conditions?"

"Whether there are rules about partners getting involved with other partners' family members."

"This ain't the agency," said Razor, slapping me on the back. "The only rules we have are, try your damnedest to stay alive while, at the same time, making sure your teammates do too."

"Then, I'm in."

A week later, after Razor and Ava's wedding, Dutch and I were each offered junior partnerships with K19 and were tapped to remain on Ava's detail in Yachats.

Doc told us the firm owned a fully furnished house in town that we could share.

"There are two bedrooms, but only one of you will be there at a time since you'll be covering twenty-four hours of detail between you."

Having the additional support gave me a lot more free time, but I wasn't sure how long it would last. Things were heating up with Petrov.

Through our contacts at MI6, the K19 team learned that Raketa Ivashov, the Russian who had helped us find Ava, her sister, and their two friends, and who Razor still believed had shot him, was thought to have been kidnapped by Petrov that same night.

Gunner and a high-ranking agent from MI6 were on their way to Azerbaijan, where Petrov was reported to be. Their mission was relatively simple, but it would put both agents in a great deal of danger. Not only were they breaking into Petrov's purported compound in the old city in order to rescue Ivashov, but they also intended to assassinate Petrov at the same time.

Dutch usually preferred taking the evening detail, and while I never stayed over, I had dinner with Saylor and the girls almost every night after Dutch relieved me.

School was back in session, and it seemed to me that both Savannah and Sierra had an inordinate amount of homework for being in the second and third grade.

"You don't have to stay and help. I've got this," Saylor said on more than one occasion when she'd found me at the table, helping the girls get through the assignments they brought home.

"I like doing it. It relaxes me," I told her one night after the girls had gone to bed.

"Cooking, dishes, and homework all relax you. You're every woman's dream man."

I captured her around the waist and pulled her close. "I don't care about every woman. I care about you."

While she tried to mask her reaction, I still caught it. She'd visibly bristled. I left shortly after that, and instead of going back to the house where Dutch and I stayed, I went over to Razor's.

"Got a minute?" I asked, coming down to the basement where Dutch was studying the monitors that surveilled the house and property.

"What can I do for you?" he asked, stretching his arms above his head.

"Want to switch for a while? I'll take nights."

"Sure…" It was obvious Dutch wanted to ask why, but the man refrained, and I appreciated it.

The schedule switch only lasted three days. The evening of the fourth, Gunner called my cell right before I was supposed to relieve Dutch.

"Change in duty," he said. "I need you on the East Coast for a few days. You can arrange your own transport, but I need you here tomorrow."

"Roger that, sir," I responded.

"Do you even want to know what the assignment is?" Gunner asked.

"Does it matter?"

When Gunner laughed and ended the call, I went in search of Dutch and found him downstairs, working out in the basement gym.

"Can you stick around a while longer?"

"Sure. All night?"

I shook my head. "Maybe just an hour."

Dutch picked up his towel and ran up the stairs. "Give me five for a shower, and then you can head out."

10

I was sitting out on the deck, enjoying the last few warm nights as summer came to an end, when I saw Monk walking on the trail, headed my way.

Relief coursed through my veins at the sight of him. Something had happened between us last week, and I still wasn't certain what it was.

"Hey," I said, standing to greet him.

"Got a minute?"

I invited him inside. "Can I get you a drink?"

"Wine would be nice, thanks."

I brought the wine in and sat next to him on the sofa.

"I've been given a new assignment, and I don't know how long I'll be away."

I had enough experience with my brother to know better than to ask Monk where he was going.

"I also wanted to apologize for being MIA."

"What happened, Monk? I don't even know."

"I made you uncomfortable when I said I didn't care about other women, only you."

I rested against the back of the sofa and looked up at the ceiling. "It wasn't a big deal."

Monk stroked his finger down my cheek; I raised my head to look at him.

"Do you know if you'll be coming back to Yachats?"

"I will."

I stood; sitting still was too difficult. "I don't like this part."

Monk stood too. "Which part?"

"It's something my mom and I always say when Razor leaves. We know we can't ask where he's going, and we know we won't hear from him while he's gone. It's the waiting and wondering part that's the hardest."

"I'm going to the East Coast."

I smiled. "You're not supposed to tell me that."

"Give me credit for knowing what I can and can't tell you."

"When do you leave?"

"Tomorrow."

I squared my shoulders. "Thank you for coming over to let me know."

When Monk stalked toward me, I knew what he would do, and even though my girls were asleep in the other room, I couldn't bring myself to stop him.

He pushed me back against the wall and grasped my neck. He brought his lips to mine and kissed me hard.

"Monk, please…" As much as I wanted to ask him to stay tonight, to share my bed one last time before he had to leave, I couldn't do it. If one of the girls woke up in the night and needed their mama, either one of them would come crawl under the covers with me. Monk couldn't be in my bed if that happened.

I kissed him again.

Monk let me go and walked over to the door. "I'll see you soon, Saylor."

I locked the door behind him, turned on the security system, and turned off all the lights. I stood near the sliding door that led out to the deck, and watched. Monk stood out on the trail between my house and Razor's, watching the ocean, or maybe he was looking at the stars. All I knew for sure was that he was in as much pain as I was.

—*Monk*—

When I arrived at the ferry launch on Chesapeake Bay, Gunner was waiting.

"I'm going back to Azerbaijan," he said. "Petrov is holding someone else prisoner there." I'd heard that

Gunner had successfully extracted the former Russian assassin from Petrov's compound but that the team didn't have the opportunity to assassinate the man himself. "Your job is to stay on the island with Raketa and keep her safe."

"Understood." I hadn't known that Gunner brought the Russian here, but that really wasn't any of my business.

"She doesn't know I'm leaving, or where I'm going, and I don't want her to."

"Roger that," I responded.

Gunner reviewed the logistics of staying on the private island, briefed me on the security systems that would need to be activated, and told me which room to stay in. He also told me that when I wasn't sleeping, to make myself scarce while, at the same time, ensuring I knew where Raketa was every minute of every day.

I didn't have a problem with any of it. In fact, I had a lot of thinking to do, and this type of assignment would give me plenty of time to do it.

"Petrov ghosted and took everyone with him," said Gunner, sounding defeated when he called several days later. "He was there one day, and by the time we got there the next, he was long gone."

"What's the next step?" I asked.

"I'm coming back, but I need you to brief Raketa before I get there."

I took notes, and when I went inside, handed them to her rather than giving her a verbal briefing. Maybe it wasn't the right way to do it, but it was likely she preferred it that way. If I were in her shoes, I would've.

Before our call ended, Gunner told me he'd be back sometime in the next few days and to expect his text. When I received it, I was to return to the mainland and Gunner would head back to the island.

From there, I was to report directly to Montecito, the town on the Central Coast of California where K19 headquarters were located.

I'd hoped I'd have time to go back to Yachats for at least a couple of days, but it didn't look as though that was going to happen.

11

"Are you okay?"

"I'm fine," I told Poppy, who I'd foolishly agreed to meet at one of the downtown bars for happy hour. When I'd stepped inside and saw the place was packed, I almost turned around and left. This so wasn't my scene. I hadn't thought it was Poppy's anymore either.

"Let's go outside."

I picked up my glass of wine and followed my friend to the bar's back patio.

"This is much better." Poppy motioned to two open chairs. "Can you believe we used to do this every Friday?"

"We did not."

"I'm pretty sure we did."

"Your brain is addled. What are you drinking?"

"It's called a Peach Cobbler. It's peach moonshine and orange juice. Wanna try it?"

"God, no. How many have you had?"

"Just this one. I'm not exactly the party girl I once was."

I couldn't figure out where all these party-every-Friday-night-girl memories were coming from. It certainly wasn't me that Poppy had gone out with.

"Have you heard from Monk?" Poppy asked when the only other two people on the patio went inside.

"No, and I didn't expect to." He'd been gone two weeks when Razor suddenly left too. "I probably should be spending more time with Ava, but her mother and sister are living here now. I'm sure she's busy with them."

Poppy took another sip of her drink. "God, this is good."

"Order another. I'll drive you home."

"Thanks, but I know better. I'll feel like death tomorrow if I do." She set the glass down on the table between us. "I've rethought my request for you to hook me up with someone who works for Razor. I can't be the woman who sits around, waiting for her spy-boyfriend to show up once every six months after flitting all over the world, doing God knows what."

"Are you suggesting I'm that woman?"

"Settle down. No, I'm not. I'm just saying I can't do it."

There'd been a time, not long after my divorce was final, when Razor sat me down and told me all the reasons why getting involved with any one of the guys he worked with would be a terrible idea.

I'd hit right back at him, saying that his breed of egotistical alpha protectors held no interest for me whatsoever. Stupid famous last words.

"They're all just so hot. You know what I mean?"

"It's a powerful combination. They're mysterious, all of them are ripped like bodybuilders, and they protect the world from the bad guys. Hard not to fall for one of them."

"I would've bet a million dollars your brother would never get married."

"I would've been right there with you."

"But he did. Some of them do, right? Do you think you and Monk—"

"No! Whatever you're about to ask, the answer is a resounding no. In fact, when he does come back—if he comes back—I'm going to tell him I'm not interested in seeing him anymore."

"Good luck with that."

"What do you mean?"

"You'd be lying, because you are interested in seeing him. Maybe just tell him you're not built for the life your brother lives. That would be closer to the truth."

I thought about her suggestion. It was a valid point. If I lied at all, Monk would pick up on it.

"How are the doodlebugs?"

I sighed. I wasn't the only one who missed Monk. They did too. Instead of constantly asking when they could visit "Aunt Ava," they now asked when he'd be back. Two days ago, I'd snapped at them about it and ended up in tears over it after they'd gone to bed.

"They miss him. Ask about him all the time."

"What do you tell them?"

"I thought about telling them he wasn't coming back, but I decided I'd probably go to hell for it. So I just told them I didn't know."

"You miss him too, Saylor."

I took a sip of wine, wondering if I should've ordered something stronger.

"It doesn't matter. Either way, this thing ends. He has no reason to spend time in Yachats."

"He doesn't?"

"None whatsoever."

"Then, what is he doing here?"

"What?"

When Poppy motioned over my head, I turned around. Monk was standing right behind me.

"Hi."

"Hi, Saylor."

"Excuse me," said Poppy.

"You don't have to leave," I said when she bent down to kiss my cheek.

"Sure, I do." Poppy walked over to Monk and introduced herself. "I've heard a lot about you."

Monk looked at her briefly, mumbled something I couldn't hear, then stalked toward me.

I stood, but before I could say a word, Monk crushed his mouth to mine. He wrapped his arms around me and pulled my body flush with his. When I tried to break the kiss, he put his hand on the side of my face and held me there, thrusting his tongue deeper into my mouth.

When I whimpered, he finally let go and rested his forehead against mine. My lips felt swollen from the pressure of his kiss.

"What did you hear, Monk?"

"Does it matter?"

I took a step back. "It does. Why did you kiss me like that?"

He wrapped his arm around my waist and pulled me back into him. "I kissed you like that because I've spent every minute since I've been gone thinking about it."

"About kissing me?"

"Everything about you."

I put my hand on his arm. "Let me go, Monk."

He released me, and I took another step back. His eyes bored into mine, and as much as I wished he'd tell me what he was thinking, another part of me didn't want to know.

"Where are the girls?"

"At the cabin with my mother."

When he took a tentative step closer, I wanted to take a step back, but stood my ground. He brushed my hair from the side of my face. "I have to ask you a question."

"Go ahead."

"Are you pulling away from me in fear, Saylor? If you tell me you're afraid of me, I'll leave now. No more questions, and you'll never see me again."

His voice was soft, and he was being so gentle.

"I'm not afraid of you, Monk. I know you'd never hurt me."

"I'd sooner die."

"I know that."

He stroked his finger down the side of my face. "Tell me why, then?"

"I missed you."

"I see," he answered, bringing my head to rest on his chest. "We've both gone against our word."

I wrapped my arms around his waist.

"Come. We'll have dinner," he said, taking my hand.

"I'd rather just go back to the house."

"We'll end up in bed."

I walked toward the bar, not letting go of his hand. We wound our way through the crowded room and out the front door.

"Did you drive?" I asked.

Monk pointed to the motorcycle parked nearby.

I couldn't explain why, but the sight of it rankled me. There was so much I didn't know about the man who held my hand in his. I knew his name and that he was from the South, but not where exactly. I knew nothing about his family or his history or even that he had a motorcycle.

I could say I based my trust in him on the fact that he worked for my brother, but that would be a lie. For the second time in my life, I'd fallen for a man solely by trusting my own instincts. The promises I'd made to myself, even my assurances to my brother and my best friend, were lies too.

"I can't do this. It's over, Monk."

He looked into my eyes a long time without speaking. I should've walked away, but I couldn't bring myself to.

"Say something. Anything."

When he stepped forward and gripped my neck, I expected him to kiss me like he had earlier. Instead, he kissed my forehead, released me, and walked over to his motorcycle.

I watched, incredulous that he would leave without a word. He didn't get on the bike, though. He took something out of the saddle bag, walked back over, and held it out.

"What is it?"

"It's a gift, Saylor. Please take it."

I let him place the soft bundle in my hand and watched him walk back to the bike.

"Thank you," I said after him, but doubted he heard. I walked to my car, trying to decide whether to go straight home or drive to the cabin where my mom and the girls were, so I wouldn't have to be alone.

I set the package next to me, put on my seat belt, and started the engine. I was about to back up when I saw Monk had pulled the motorcycle up next to me. I turned the car off, unfastened my seat belt, opened the door, and got out.

"What just happened?" he asked, getting off the bike and walking over to me.

"I don't know anything about you."

"What do you want to know?"

"That isn't the point."

He stood close but didn't touch me. "What's the point, Saylor?"

"I said I wouldn't do this. I don't want this."

"This? What's between us?"

"Yes." I stepped forward and rested my head against his chest. Monk put his arms around me and rested his head against mine.

"You know me better than you think," he murmured.

"I don't know where you grew up."

"Just outside Nashville, in a place called Franklin."

"Does your family still live there?"

I could feel him shake his head. "I don't have any family left. My mother died five years ago while I was undercover."

"I'm so sorry."

"Saylor, look at me." I raised my head. "Whatever you want to know, all you have to do is ask."

"Have you ever been married?"

"No."

"Children?"

He smiled. "Before I met your girls, I would've said that kids don't like me."

"Come back to the house with me."

"Are you sure?"

"I'll ask more questions."

—Monk—

I followed on the motorcycle, stopping in the drive-way when Saylor pulled her Jeep into the garage.

"There's room for your bike," she said, motioning with her hand.

I started the motorcycle back up and pulled into the open space.

"What is it?" she asked when I climbed off and set my helmet on the seat.

"A Ducati Scrambler."

"I like it."

I followed her inside.

"Wine?"

"I'm good."

"Mind if I have a glass?"

"Not at all," I said, taking the bottle from her hand to open it.

"I can do that."

"I like doing things for you."

I followed Saylor out onto the deck, lit the fire pit, and sat down next to her on the outdoor sofa. She snuggled against me when I put my arm around her. I closed my eyes, remembering how I felt only a half hour ago, thinking that I might never feel her body against mine again.

She reached up and put her hand on my heart, as though she knew I was re-experiencing the pain.

"Was your mother your only family?"

I opened my eyes and looked out at the water. "I had a sister."

Saylor sat up, turning so she faced me. "You said that at the hospital. I forgot. What happened to her?"

There were very few people who knew the story, and it was a long time since I'd told it. I took a deep breath. "Men broke into the house, probably to rob it. They found her in the kitchen, and they killed her."

Saylor put her arms around me and rested her head on my chest like she had before. "I'm so sorry, Monk."

I put my hand on her arm. "I need to show you something."

She sat up. "Okay."

I lifted my shirt, took her hand, and brought the tips of her fingers to the center of one of my tattoos—the Aztec sun—the same one her brother had.

"What is that?" she asked, as her fingers traced the scar.

"I was shot too."

Saylor put her other hand over her mouth, and her eyes met mine.

"They didn't just kill her. They raped her first."

"Oh my God," she whispered. "You were there."

"I was eleven."

Her eyes filled with tears. "I don't know what to say."

I opened her hand so her fingers were splayed over the sun. "When we were at the hospital, you said you didn't know me then, too."

"I remember."

"Do you remember what I said?"

"I do. You said 'sure, you do.' You also asked me if I believe in angels."

I looked up at the sky and closed my eyes, knowing that what I was about to say would sound crazy. "She told me not to let you go. Back in the parking lot."

"Your sister?"

"Yes."

"Let's go inside now."

"Are you cold?" I asked.

"No."

I stood when Saylor did, turned the fire off, and followed her inside. She locked the patio door and reached to turn off the light.

12

I rolled over in bed. Something was different this morning. I could smell coffee. And bacon. Monk was here. He'd spent the night last night. I'd gone from breaking things off with him to mind-blowing sex in the span of a couple of hours.

Instead of getting out of bed, I stayed where I was, trying to decide whether to spend the time analyzing the decisions I made or just go with the flow of life.

Was there really any point in doing the former? I liked Monk. A lot, actually. I knew I could trust him; the man worked for my brother. My guess was Rhys "Monk" Perrin had been fully vetted prior to K19 giving him his first assignment and then went through another round when Razor found out Monk and I were spending time together. If he'd had any secrets whatsoever, K19 would've uncovered every last one of them.

I was just about to get up, grab my robe, and join Monk in the kitchen when he walked in with a tray of coffee, food, and flowers.

"You're spoiling me."

Monk set the tray on the bed and climbed in next to me. "I like doing things for you."

"I haven't done anything for you."

"I disagree, but if you'd like to, I have some ideas." He wiggled his eyebrows in a very un-Monk-like manner.

I grabbed a piece of perfectly prepared bacon from the single yet heavily laden plate on the tray and took a bite.

"You're very easygoing, Monk."

He shook his head. "I am the opposite."

"With me, you are."

"Only with you."

I took a sip of coffee. "Thank you for making breakfast."

He studied me.

"What?"

He shook his head.

"What's on your mind, Monk?"

"I…"

I turned to my side and propped my head on my hand. "Talk to me, oh, Quiet One."

He grinned. "The pain I felt last night…"

"I felt it too."

He leaned forward and kissed me. The man was an expert at it. I pushed any thoughts of who he'd practiced with out of my head and touched the silver ball on his tongue with the tip of mine. He broke our kiss, stood, moved the tray off the bed, and picked up one of the condoms we'd left on the bedside table.

I threw the covers off my body and watched as he pushed his shorts to the floor.

"I love looking at you." I smiled when he stood where he was, letting me, while at the same time, trailing his eyes over my nakedness.

When I held my hand out to him, Monk took it and sat on the edge of the bed.

"I want this with you."

"I want it too, Monk. I just don't know how to define what 'this' is."

He rested his hand on my thigh, his fingers creeping maddeningly close to my heated core. I reached up and put my hand on his shoulder, pulling him toward me. "Kiss me again."

He did and held my face in his hands. "I have to leave in the morning."

"I think I knew that."

"I don't know when I'll be back."

"I knew that too."

—*Monk*—

The breakfast I'd made for Saylor was now cold, but she didn't seem to mind. Her hunger for food matched the hunger I'd had for her body in the last hour.

I loved how easily she smiled, how often she touched me, even if it was just to rest her hand somewhere on my body. At the moment, her left hand was on my thigh, right above my knee, while she continued to eat with her right.

Last night, I'd shared the story of my sister's death with her and I'd briefly mentioned my mother's passing. I hadn't said a word about my father; she hadn't asked, and I was glad of it. If she had, I would've had to talk about the abuse my mom had suffered at his hands, which would serve as a reminder of Saylor's ex-husband. When the time was right, I would tell her that story too. I had to. I couldn't keep my father's murder a secret and truly hold myself open to her. Saylor would sense that I was keeping something back, and when she did, her insecurity would lead her to make assumptions that weren't accurate.

"I'd ask what you're thinking about, but I know that look."

I raised my eyebrows and studied her.

"Razor goes to the same place you are right now. There are memories he'll carry with him for the rest of his life. Things I know he wonders if he could've done differently. And while he never talks to me about it, I can sense what he's going through. I'll tell you the same thing I would tell him if I ever have the opportunity."

"What is that?"

"The decisions you make are the best ones given the circumstances of the situation you're in. There is a positive byproduct that comes with second-guessing, feeling regret, questioning yourself or your actions; it will help you make the same decisions in the future with less hesitation."

"Insightful."

Saylor got up to go into the bathroom. "Or full of shit."

"Insightful," I repeated, laughing.

When I picked up the breakfast tray, Saylor stuck her head out the door. "I know doing dishes relaxes you, but showering with you relaxes me."

I set the tray back on the bed and joined her, grateful that she so often told me what she wanted rather than expect me to guess.

*

"Where are you headed?" Onyx asked three weeks later when we'd finished our hotwash of the final Petrov op.

I checked the time. "I'll find a place to crash and catch a flight in the morning."

"To?" Onyx asked, looking down on me. I wasn't short by anyone's yardstick, yet Onyx was taller. How a six-foot-six guy ever piloted the fighter jets Onyx had was something I'd never been able to wrap my head around.

"Oregon."

"We're scheduled to fly out at zero six hundred."

My primary concern had been getting the earliest flight out I could, but there wasn't a commercial flight leaving that early. "Roger that. I'll fly out with you."

"I'm headed up to the plane now if you want to catch a ride."

"I need sleep."

Onyx rolled his eyes. "Shit, I shoulda thought of that too since I'm flyin' the aircraft tomorrow."

I shook my head. "Yeah, I'll go. Thanks."

We went back into the main room of Doc and Merrigan Butler's house, which also served as K19 headquarters and where those who had been part of the op were gathered. I had to admit, it was the nicest house I'd ever been in. Although from what I'd seen, all four of the founding K19 partners had pretty nice digs; Gunner owned his own fucking island.

"Any word on Alegria?" Onyx asked after reporting that he and I were headed to the airfield.

"Still in surgery," Doc answered. "I'll keep you posted."

"This was a rough one," said Onyx once we were on our way to the airfield just north, in Santa Barbara.

I agreed. It had taken agents and officers from three international intelligence agencies to join ranks to take down one man, Makar Petrov—aka Conor McNamara—father to Razor's wife, Ava, her twin sister, Aine, and as we'd learned tonight, Raketa Ivashov. The man had intended to kill all three of his offspring in order to get his hands on trust funds worth millions of dollars that he'd set up in each of their names years prior.

The CIA, working in conjunction with K19, along with MI6 and the most unlikely of the trio—United Russia—had joined forces to assassinate Petrov.

In the course of the op, Alegria, who was one of K19's regular pilots and who Onyx had been flying with for years, was shot. As Doc had told us, she was in surgery, her condition unknown.

In addition to holding a hostage at gunpoint, Petrov had set up explosive devices in the area surrounding his hideout, and Onyx, a bomb expert as well as a pilot, had been called upon to diffuse them.

"I should've asked if you wanted me to drive," I muttered, feeling like an asshole for telling Onyx that I needed rest.

"We're good. The airfield is only another ten minutes away."

"Where do you sleep?"

Onyx laughed. "You think the only people who use those staterooms are the senior partners?"

"Who's your co-pilot tomorrow?"

"Corazón."

"Never met him."

"Her. Sofia 'Corazón' Descanso."

"Never met her either."

Onyx laughed. "You will in a few minutes. She's waiting at the hangar."

"I thought there were only two cabins in the back."

"You are slow as shit on the uptake tonight, man."

"You and Corazón…"

"Yeah, me and Corazón. And I gotta tell you, if there was ever a night I could use the comfort found in the arms of a hot Latina woman, it's tonight."

I understood. At least needing the comfort found in the arms of a woman. If there had been any way for me to be in Yachats tonight, I would've done so. What I would've done once I got there, I would've had to figure out.

Saylor's no-PDA-or-sleepovers rule was still fully in effect, so sneaking into her bed would've been out of the question. Calling her in the middle of the night to come to me would've been equally so.

I scrubbed my face with my hand. No matter what either of us had said going in, the bottom line was Saylor and I were both in way deep. But I couldn't see myself walking away any more than I could see her doing so.

13

"It isn't that I like it when Monk isn't here, but the truth is, I do get a lot more of your attention," said Poppy, tossing a piece of popcorn into her mouth.

"When did this popcorn obsession start?"

"What do you mean? I've always liked popcorn."

I rolled my eyes. "You bring a bag with you every time you come over. You used to bring a bottle of wine."

"Shit." Poppy looked over her shoulder and waited for Sierra or Savannah to holler at her, but neither did. "I left the wine out in the car."

She ran out and came back in, carrying a chilled bottle of red. "I guess we'll have to let this warm up a bit."

I poured a glass of the wine I already had open. "Will a Pinot do?"

"I'm not picky. You know this." Poppy took another handful of popcorn. "Do you know when he'll be back?"

"No idea, but wherever he went, he isn't alone. My brother went MIA right about the time Monk had to leave."

"Don't you get curious?"

"At times, I wonder where he is, but I don't think it's out of curiosity."

"What is it, then?"

I shrugged. "I don't know…I guess curiosity is as good a word as any."

"You miss him."

I reached into my friend's bowl and tossed a handful of kernels at her. "Don't go there."

"I have to live vicariously through you since no guy I've met interests me as much as Portland guy."

"Comparison is the killer of joy," I said, but I knew exactly what Poppy meant. I couldn't imagine any other man on the face of the earth who could hold a candle to Monk.

He was hotter than shit, edgier than anyone I'd ever dated or even considered dating, with his tattoos and his tongue piercing and his café racer motorcycle. And he was so much more than that. He was a gentleman who was great with my girls, treated me like a princess, a fabulous cook, and while he didn't talk a lot, what he did say was interesting and thought-provoking. To be cliché, we clicked.

Yes, I missed him, like I'd never missed anyone before. I longed to feel Monk next to me every night that I climbed in bed alone. I found myself daydreaming about him as I made morning coffee and when I made dinner for myself and the girls.

That they asked about him daily didn't help. Nor did my mother's incessant teasing about how I had finally found someone man enough to hold my interest.

I sighed and looked over at Poppy, who held her bowl of popcorn on her lap, taking handful after handful while she zoned out on what looked like the most compelling movie she'd ever seen. Except her eyes were glued to me, and my friend had just seen every memory play out on my face.

"You're in love," said Poppy.

"I'm in lust," I countered.

"Nope. That look isn't lust. That is full-blown, all-out, heart-and-soul love." My friend tapped her lower lip with her finger. "Wanna know how I know?"

I sighed. "Sure."

"Because I've never seen you look like this."

I had to concede that I'd never felt about Cliff the way I did just now, thinking about Monk. And it terrified me.

I saw two big black SUVs pull up to my brother's house and wondered if Monk was in one of them. There was a chance that he wasn't even with the group, but something told me he was.

I was standing on tiptoes, peering out the kitchen window, when something, or someone, caught my eye on the deck. I smiled, knowing that I'd been caught when Monk, standing just outside the door, winked.

Racing over, I unlocked it, and in a move that was, in the hindsight of a split second, probably an overreaction, launched myself into his arms.

"I missed you," I admitted, backing away.

Monk snaked his arm around my waist and pulled my body flush with his. "Don't be embarrassed." He gave me one of his scorchingly hot kisses.

Without breaking our kiss, he gripped my bottom with his big hands and lifted me so my legs were wrapped around his waist.

"Where are the girls?"

"School."

He reached around and closed the door that led from the deck into the house with one hand while he held my body next to his with the other. He carried me into the bedroom, grinding his hardness against me.

"I missed you too." He set me on my feet and pulled my shirt over my head. "Drop your hands," he said when I reached around to unfasten my bra.

Monk's demanding tone sent a shudder down the length of my body. If he weren't holding me up, my knees would've buckled.

He pulled the cup of my bra below my breast and sucked my nipple into his mouth. Pain and pleasure melded into one as he sucked hard and bit the sensitive, hardened flesh.

"Saylor." He groaned before turning his assault on my other breast.

"When do the girls get home?" he asked.

"Three," I answered, looking over at the clock on the bedside table. Had four hours really passed since Monk arrived at my back door?

"Come," he said, easing himself off the bed. He held out his hand, led me into the bathroom, turned on the shower, and adjusted the temperature before ushering me under the warm stream of water.

"Close your eyes."

"Monk?"

"Yes, Saylor."

"Um…what are you doing for Thanksgiving?"

"Close your eyes," he said again as he drizzled shampoo into his palm and waited for me to do as I was told before continuing. "I don't give much thought to holidays."

"Ava told me that she and Razor are planning to spend it in Cambria."

I opened my eyes again when he didn't say anything. He leaned forward and touched my lips with his. "Are you asking me to spend Thanksgiving with you?"

"I guess I am."

"I'd enjoy that."

"It isn't too much? I mean, it's a holiday."

Monk gave me an indulgent smile. "Stop overthinking things, Saylor. I enjoy spending time with you and the girls."

"We enjoy spending time with you too."

"Close your eyes. Stop thinking. Just feel."

He massaged my scalp, his fingers digging in just enough to make me groan.

"I like that sound," he said, moving from my scalp, down my neck to my shoulders.

I groaned again. "That feels so good."

When his hands left my body, I wanted to cry. I opened my eyes and watched as he lathered up the body wash. When Monk raised a brow, I smirked and closed my eyes.

"Good girl," he muttered, bringing his soapy hands to my breasts. He lifted their weight in each hand and massaged them the same way he had my shoulders. I couldn't stop myself from groaning again.

I felt his breath near my ear. "I dreamed about you making those sexy-as-fuck noises."

He wrapped one arm around my waist as though he anticipated my knees buckling. His other hand trailed to the heat between my legs. While his fingers ran through my folds, his tongue circled my nipples with the cold ball on its tip. I gripped his shoulders as my body clenched in another mind-blowing orgasm. I lost count of how many I'd had in the last few hours. It was almost as though all it took was just having his hands, his mouth, his hardness touch me.

—Monk—

A few days later, I sat on Razor's deck and raised my face to the sun. A day as warm as this on the Oregon Coast was rare, and it felt good. I loved heat. The hotter, the better, usually. Being with Saylor, though, feeling her warmth, made tolerating the colder climate easier.

I closed my eyes, letting my thoughts drift to earlier in the week when I'd pressed myself deep inside of her. I'd been away from Saylor for a handful of days, and yet my release was as strong as if I hadn't had sex in several weeks.

The sliding door opened, and Razor joined me.

"Damn, it's almost hot out here. Want one?"

I turned my head. "Thanks," I said, taking the bottle of beer Razor offered.

"I was going to ask if you needed time off for the holidays, but Avarie said you'd be in Cambria with us for Thanksgiving."

"Yes."

Razor shook his head and laughed. "You're the perfect man for my sister. You never talk and she never stops."

"I haven't found that to be true."

When Razor raised his eyebrow and smirked, I shook my head and laughed.

"You're welcome to tell me it's none of my damn business, but Saylor…" Razor took a deep breath. "I don't know how much you know about her ex, but he hurt her pretty bad. Not just physically, but emotionally too. The physical shit is why I took care of getting the fucker put in prison the minute I had enough on him."

"I know."

"How serious—"

I held up my hand, and Razor stopped talking.

"None of my business, is that what you're saying?"

"Yes. What your sister does is her business."

"You understand if you hurt her, I'll kill you."

"If I learned anyone had, I'd kill them too."

"What about Sierra and Savannah? They're a package deal."

I stared out at the ocean. "I understand."

"Saylor's staying at the house with us in Cambria."

"Yes."

Razor leaned forward and rested his elbows on his knees. "Where are you staying, Monk?"

"I've reserved a room."

Razor stood, took a long swig of his beer, and then patted my shoulder. "Good talk," he said before going back inside.

I closed my eyes again, raising my face to the sun. Where the horrors of my job once resided, Saylor had taken their place. My visions weren't of missions and death; they were of her. I smiled, knowing at that very moment, she'd be fretting over what spending Thanksgiving together meant. Given I'd seen her friend's car in the driveway, my guess was that Poppy was getting an earful.

There hadn't been any talk of new missions lately, not since the Petrov assassination, but I knew there soon would be. There was too much evil in the world to think that the K19 crew wouldn't soon be called upon to eliminate some of it.

When that happened or, more importantly, after it was over, it wasn't likely I would be needed here in Yachats any longer. It was a reality both Saylor and I would have to face. It wouldn't be easy for either of us, but I was more worried about Sierra and Savannah. They'd grown as attached to me as I was to them. When the time came for me to move on, they'd be hurt, and I regretted that.

I heard the slider open again.

"There was one other thing, Monk," said Razor, sitting in the chair next to me.

"What's that?"

"Since it seems like your base is going to be Yachats, I'm just wondering if you want to start looking for another place to live. The K19 house was intended more as a crash pad or safe house if we needed one. Don't misunderstand; you're welcome to stay there as long as you'd like. I just wanted to let you know that you don't have to."

"Copy that," I said, taking the last swig of beer and wishing Razor had brought another one out with him.

This time when Razor went back inside and I closed my eyes, the sun's warmth did nothing to quell the uncomfortable feeling that had settled in my chest. Finding another place to live, even having Razor say that it seemed like Yachats would be my base, was the opposite of what I'd just been thinking about.

I'd never intended for Oregon to be my home, Saylor or no Saylor. Finding a place to live here would send an entirely different message; one I wasn't ready to send.

If no missions were scheduled by mid-January, I'd have to talk to someone about where I did intend to be based out of, and that someone couldn't be Saylor's brother.

14

—Saylor—

"You're welcome to come with us," I told Poppy, who was currently sitting in the kitchen, pouting. "Cambria's a beautiful place to spend Thanksgiving, plus it will be fun."

"How pathetic would that be?"

"On a scale of one to ten? Negative five."

"That's pretty damn pathetic."

"You know that isn't how I meant it."

"It's your first Thanksgiving with Monk. You don't want me intruding on that."

I bit my bottom lip. When I asked what he was doing for the holiday, I'd meant it to be more of a "you're welcome to come along with us" invitation than a "this is our first Thanksgiving together" invitation. Based on Poppy's reaction as well as Razor's, it seemed like it was more of a thing than I wanted it to be.

"What are you thinking about?" Poppy asked.

"Maybe I should uninvite him."

"Saylor, you can't do that!"

"It was supposed to be casual."

"Then, talk to him about it, but don't uninvite him."

Nodding but not convinced, I made a plan to talk to Monk tonight, even though I intended to do the very thing Poppy told me not to.

"I've been thinking about Thanksgiving," I began after the girls had gone into their bedroom for the night.

"As have I."

My eyes opened wide. "What have you been thinking?"

Monk rested his hand on my thigh. "The same thing you have."

"It's more than either of us want."

"More than we said we wanted."

"Monk…"

Reaching forward, he cupped my cheek. "This isn't something we need to talk about. Let's enjoy the time we have together. Next year, things will be changing drastically."

While the same things had been racing through my head, hearing Monk say them, hurt more than I expected. "In what way?"

"I won't be working in Yachats after the first of the year."

"Oh." Before the tears I knew were coming filled my eyes, I got up and went into the kitchen. Monk followed, and when I rested my hands on the edge of the kitchen counter, he stood behind me and wrapped his arms around my waist.

"I feel the same way you do, Saylor. I love spending time with you, but we both—"

"You don't need to say anything else. When you leave, this will be over." I wiggled out of his grasp and walked out of the kitchen. "Good night, Monk."

I didn't look back to see if he left. He always left. The no-sleepover rule was still in effect.

—Monk—

I'd lied to Saylor right before Thanksgiving, but now that Christmas was almost here, my lie had become the truth. I'd spoken to Doc before agreeing to spend the holiday in Annapolis at Gunner's mother's place. Most of the K19 team would be there, as would Saylor, her girls, and Sally.

Things between Saylor and I had gone back to as normal as possible. I didn't eat dinner with them every night, and when I did, I didn't always stay to help the girls with their homework.

They were smart kids and knew something was up between their mother and me. Sadness lurked behind their little eyes, but I couldn't do anything to help that. Saylor and I were in agreement. While we cared about each other, neither wanted a long-term relationship.

She put on a brave face in front of everyone but me. As far as even Razor knew, nothing had changed between us. She was quick to smile, laughed heartily, and flirted with me in the same way she always had. Sex, though, had changed. Saylor had pulled away from me to the point where she no longer scheduled sleepovers for the girls.

When we kissed, my body longed to feel hers next to me. I wanted nothing more than to bury myself deep inside her warmth and never leave. Wanting that and making it happen were two very different things. Even if I told Saylor that I'd changed my mind and planned to stay in Yachats, I was only half of the equation. She hadn't said she wanted me to. She'd only said that when I did leave, this thing between us would be over.

Maybe the truth neither of us wanted to acknowledge was that it had run its course anyway.

15

The first few days into the new year, after Monk left on a mission with my brother, were the hardest of my life.

Monk and I had agreed to tell the girls he needed to leave because of his job, but he'd see them soon. Maybe that hadn't been the best way to handle it, but seeing my girls heartbroken over him leaving permanently was too hard. My own heartbreak was devastating enough.

"I hate to see you like this," my mother said a week into what I knew would be forever. "Couldn't the two of you have worked something out?"

"Monk never signed up to be the father figure in an insta-family, Mom. What was I going to do? Beg him to do something he'd never agreed to just because the girls and I grew attached to him?"

"You could've told him how you feel."

"To what end? All that would've done is make him feel worse about his decision. I couldn't bear to think he was here with us out of pity."

"Maybe he feels the same way you do. Maybe he's as afraid to say it as you are."

I shook my head. "Monk doesn't lie, nor does he say things that aren't necessary. I heard him, Mom. It's as over as this conversation is."

My mom breathed a heavy sigh. "So what are you going to do with your life, Saylor? Sit around and mope every day?"

"Nope. I'm going to do what I should've done years ago. I'm going to get my pilot's license."

"Glad to hear it," she said. I just wished it was with a little more enthusiasm.

Part 2

16

—Saylor—
October

"Tabon is really proud of you," said Ava as she nursed Sam. It was hard for me to believe my nephew was already three months old. It seemed as though it was only yesterday that we celebrated his arrival on the Fourth of July.

Tabon Samuel Sharp VI was as much of a force to be reckoned with as his father had been in his first six months—and Ava handled it with a finesse I didn't possess. I hadn't seen my sister-in-law get frustrated with Sam's fussiness a single time, not that I was able to be here with them as much as I'd like.

In the last ten months, I'd completed the flight training necessary and passed the exams to earn my private pilot's license. I was almost halfway through completing the two hundred and fifty hours I needed in order to sit for the commercial pilot's license exam.

I'd never be able to thank my mother and Poppy enough for how often they stepped in to help with the girls. Whether I was in the air or studying, one or the other took the girls to and from school, music lessons, and sports practice.

During their summer break, Ya-Ya took Sierra and Savannah to the fishing cabin every week, often for several days at a time. When I was able, I joined them, but it was never as much as I'd like.

No amount of busy stopped me from thinking about Monk, though. He was still the first person I thought of when I woke and the last before I fell asleep.

I knew from Razor's schedule that he'd been away on missions almost nonstop since the beginning of the year. I didn't know where, or what they involved, and I didn't want to.

"Do you want to hold him?" Ava asked, buttoning up her blouse when she finished breastfeeding the baby.

"Do you have to ask?"

"No, but it's better than just dumping him in your lap."

"Dump away," I said, holding my arms out to take Sam. "God, when did he get so heavy? What does he weigh? Thirty pounds?"

"No, not thirty, but he was twenty at his last checkup." Ava laughed. "Just like his daddy, he's in the ninety-ninth percentile of height and weight."

I held Sam up and let him bounce on my legs. "Your arms must be very strong."

"I wimp out a lot, and Tabon has to take him." She stood and walked into the kitchen. "Can I get you anything?"

"I'm good. Just spending time with this big guy is all I need." I nuzzled his neck, and Sam giggled.

Ava came back with a glass of water and sat down. "There's something I feel like I should tell you."

"Uh-oh, are you pregnant again?"

Ava laughed out loud. "Good God, no. This is about Monk."

"It's okay—"

"He'll be here later today. Tabon said they're installing new equipment, and Monk will be setting it up."

I kept my focus on Sam, trying my hardest not to react to Ava's news. I wanted to cheer and cry at the same time. I missed him so much and couldn't wait to see him. At the same time, seeing him would be even harder than missing him. Being able to look at him but not touch would be torture.

"How long did he say he'd be here?"

Ava sighed. "He said, 'Indefinitely.'"

My heart lurched. Indefinitely? Why? Maybe I could convince Ava to bring Sam over to my place so I didn't have to come here. Right. How selfish would that be? Plus, I'd have to see him eventually. Better to rip the bandage off and get it over with. Little by little, my heart would probably mend, even though it hadn't in ten months.

"Tabon asked me a funny question."

"What was that?"

"He asked if I thought you'd want Monk to know about your pilot training. Why wouldn't you?"

I thought the question over before answering. Why wouldn't I? I had no reason, but I hesitated. "I'd rather he not know," I finally answered. "I can't explain it."

"Got it," said Ava as though she truly did.

—Monk—

Ten months. That was how long it had been since I'd seen Saylor, but the hurt of leaving her was still as strong as it had been the day I did it.

I dreamed about her every night, often waking with an erection so hard it hurt. That wasn't all I missed, though. In my dreams, it was her smile, her laughter, her voice, and her words I yearned for when I woke up disappointed that being with her again hadn't been real.

There had been countless times I wanted to ask about her, but I'd stopped myself. What right did I have to know anything about her life? We'd mutually agreed to end things. While I still held out hope that, at the very least, we could be friends, whatever she was doing with her life wasn't any of my business.

"You good with this?" Razor asked when I walked into the house I hadn't set foot in since last year.

"It's my assignment."

"I didn't ask if it was your assignment." He sounded pissed.

"I'm good with it."

"Thanks for giving me that much." He walked downstairs, scrubbing his face with his hand. "Look, I don't know what happened between you and my sister, and I don't want to know. But if you're going to have any issue being here, then I need to know right now."

"I can't lie," I began, knowing that the next words I said may very well lead to me getting a different assignment.

"Go on. What can't you lie about?"

"Saylor is a person I care about. That we can't be together isn't easy for me. I have a job to do, and I'll do it, just like any other job. I'll handle myself professionally."

"Fuck," muttered Razor. "Now, I know it's really bad."

"Why?"

"Because I've never heard you string that many words together at one time."

When Razor walked out of the room, I called Burns Butler. "I'm here, walk me through what I need to do."

Seven hours later, the components of the system were fully installed and functional. The capabilities this gave K19 were like none I'd ever seen. My understanding was that similar systems were being installed at Razor's place in Cambria and, eventually, in Doc and Merrigan's place in Montecito.

The technology Burns developed was the same as what was used with top-secret drones. My guess was that the US government had hired Burns to create their systems as well.

"Are you going to hide out down here all day and night?" Razor asked, walking into the office with a plate of food.

"Working, not hiding."

"Right. You keep tellin' yourself that. She isn't here, by the way, and I doubt we'll see much of her. She's been keeping herself pretty busy."

I felt a stabbing pain in my chest. I couldn't help but wonder if by "keeping herself busy," Razor meant she was seeing someone.

"Ask, asshole."

I stood and took the plate from Razor's hand. "Thanks for this."

"Ask," Razor repeated.

"It isn't any of my business."

"Ask anyway."

I sighed and set the plate of food on the desk. "Is she seeing someone?"

"No. So what are you going to do about it?"

I studied him. Why was Razor pushing so hard? Had Saylor talked to him? Did she want me back in her life?

He put his hand on my shoulder. "Go see her. She'll be happy you did, and so will Sierra and Savannah. They've been worried about you."

"I don't think that's a good idea."

"Why not?"

"Because, eventually, I'll leave again."

"Maybe. But maybe not."

17

Hoping to take my mind off the fact that Monk would descend on Yachats any minute, I scheduled a flight. He'd still be lurking in the back of my mind, but flying had been my escape for the last several months; it was the best therapy I'd found.

My mother had already picked the girls up from school and told me that since it was Friday night, they'd be going out for dinner followed by a sleepover.

I was about to go into the bedroom to change when I saw Monk out on the trail, headed my way. I couldn't pretend I wasn't home or that I hadn't seen him. The lights were on in my kitchen, and he was looking right at me.

I checked the time; I'd have to leave in the next five minutes or I'd miss my slot. I sent a quick text saying something had come up and that I'd have to reschedule. There'd be a fee, but what else could I do? I hadn't seen the man in almost a year.

He came up the steps to the deck where I was already waiting by the sliding door. Even with glass between us, the man sucked all the air out of my lungs.

"Hi," I said, slowly opening the door.

"Saylor."

"How are you, Monk?" I asked, motioning for him to come inside. When he did, his body brushed against mine. I shuddered.

"I felt it too." He took a step back, cupped my face with his palm, and stared into my eyes. "I want to kiss you."

I didn't give him permission, nor did I wait. I leaned forward and kissed him. When his tongue thrust into my mouth, I whimpered.

Monk pulled back. "I'm sorry—"

I put my fingertips on his lips. "Don't be. It was my fault." When I moved away from him, he grabbed my wrist, but when my eyes met his, he let go.

"I missed you so much," he murmured.

No, no, no! I wanted to shout out at him. We couldn't start up again only to have him leave in a few months. My heart couldn't take it. "Monk, I…"

"It was a mistake to walk away from you."

I turned my back to him when I felt my eyes fill with tears. "Please don't do this."

"Are you saying you didn't miss me? You don't feel the same way I do?"

I shook my head.

"Turn around and look at me, Saylor."

First, I looked up at the ceiling, willing my damn tears away, and then slowly turned around.

"Tell me you didn't miss me, and I'll walk right back out that door."

"I can't."

He stepped closer. "Can't what?"

"I can't tell you that I didn't miss you. I can't tell you that it wasn't a mistake to let you walk away, but, Monk, I can't do this again."

What were simple tears a moment ago, turned into full-blown sobbing. Every inch of me ached with longing for the man standing close enough to touch, and yet I couldn't bring myself to reach out. When he did, wrapping his arms around me, pulling me into his chest, I couldn't bring myself to back away again either.

He held me tight, and it felt so good. Too good. The way my body sank into his was like we were two puzzle pieces that fit perfectly together. I could feel his arousal, and it added to the heat already pooling in my core.

He captured my mouth with his. This time he was gentler, the kiss softer; he made love to my mouth with his. He nibbled my bottom lip and then rolled the ball on the tip of his tongue over the same place. The coolness of it soothed me.

"Come with me," he said, taking my hand and leading me through the house to the garage.

"Where are we going?" I asked.

"To dinner, and before you ask why, I'm hungrier for you than I am for food, and if we don't leave now, I'll devour you."

"I don't want food, Monk. I only want you."

He sighed and closed his eyes as though he was counting like I did when I was angry with my girls and needed time to think before I spoke.

"I missed more than being inside of you, Saylor. I need more from you first."

What I should do was pull away from him, ask him to leave, tell him again that this wasn't what I wanted, but I couldn't. His body was a magnet, and I couldn't resist its pull.

I tossed him the keys after opening the garage door. There was no way I could drive in my present state.

As he backed out the Jeep and drove downtown, I studied him. There were a few more gray hairs mixed in with the black both on his head and in his beard. The lines on his face appeared more pronounced than when I last saw him too. What had happened; what did he go through in the last ten months that had aged him in such a way that I noticed?

He looked over and smiled. "I like your eyes on me."

"I like your eyes on me too."

He reached over, took my hand, and brought it to his lips, making me wish we were still steps away from my bedroom rather than about to turn into a restaurant's parking lot.

He came around to help me out of the Jeep. Even though I didn't need it, I liked the gentlemanly side of him.

"Just one more." He brought his lips to mine. The kiss wasn't chaste by any means, but it wasn't as heated as the earlier one we'd shared either.

"Tell me what you've been doing," he said once we were seated at a table. "Razor said you've been busy."

"The usual. The girls keep me busy."

"There's more, though."

"What did Razor tell you?"

"Only that you weren't seeing anyone that he knew of."

"You asked?"

"I did."

"What about you, Monk? Have you been seeing anyone?"

He reached across the table and took my hand. "You know the answer to that."

"But why? Why haven't you been seeing anyone? And why haven't I? We agreed to end this, and look at us. The minute you're back in town, we can't keep our hands off each other." I shook my head. "Why can't I resist you, Monk?"

"The same reason I can't resist you. I dreamed of you every night and in my daydreams too. It didn't diminish, Saylor. My longing for you only intensified."

"We're crazy." I took my hand back and opened the menu. "I suppose part of our being civilized requires we share a meal, although no matter how much I eat, I'll still remain as hungry as I am now." I said all of that without looking at him. When I was finally able to meet his gaze, he looked as though he was on fire with want for me, just like I was for him.

"Nothing will change, Monk. You'll still leave again, and my heart will shatter. Not just mine, my girls' too. I was cleaning their room the other day and found a calendar that Savannah had hidden under her bed. She's marked every day you've been gone with a big red X."

"If I leave, your heart will shatter?"

My cheeks flushed. I had said that out loud, hadn't I? I tried to study the menu, but everything was a blur.

Monk got up from the table, came around, and sat in the chair next to mine. "My heart will shatter if I leave again too."

"But you have to leave. Yachats isn't your base. There are missions or ops or whatever you call them, and when they're over, you have to go home." I shook my head. "I don't even know where your home is, Monk."

"If I agreed to make Yachats my home, then I would return after each one, just like your brother does."

"Are you saying that's what you want to do?"

"I see no other option."

"Does this mean we're going to be in a relationship, Monk? We both said we weren't looking for one."

"Sometimes, things appear whether you're looking for them or not."

"I don't know."

"As I said, I see no other option."

"You make it sound so…businesslike."

"This isn't like you, Saylor," he said, stroking my cheek with his finger. I leaned over and put my head on his shoulder.

"I'm sorry. It's been…rough."

"For me too." He put his finger under my chin and brought his lips to mine.

I moved so my mouth was close to his ear. "I'm scared," I whispered.

"As am I." Monk backed away and scrubbed his face with his hand. "There's something we need to talk about."

I looked into his eyes. "Okay."

"Not here. Later, but before we go back to your house."

"You're worrying me a little, Monk. Can you give me any idea what it's about?"

"I need to tell you about my father."

—*Monk*—

Saylor ate very little of her dinner, not that I expected her to eat much, particularly after dropping the bomb about needing to talk about my father. I had no idea why I'd brought it up like I had, or even why it suddenly became so urgent that I tell her about what happened. All I knew was if we were going to make a commitment of any kind to each other, she needed to know about the second thing that had contributed to me becoming the man I was today.

I'd already told her about my sister, and as hard as that story had been to get out, this one was more difficult. Instead of driving Saylor back to her place, I parked the Jeep on one of the scenic overlooks that dotted the Yachats highway.

"My father wasn't around a lot when I was growing up," I began, looking out at the ocean rather than at her. "What I found out when I was a teenager, a few years after my sister's death, was that he'd spent most of his time away from us in prison. My mother never wanted us to know, so she said nothing."

"I do the same thing with my girls," Saylor said as though she was defending my mother's actions.

"You're right to, particularly given their age."

"What was he in prison for?"

"All kinds of stuff. Armed robbery, drug trafficking. He wasn't a very good man. After my sister died, he got worse."

Saylor turned in her seat so she was looking directly at me. I couldn't do the same.

"What happened?"

"It could've been that I was older and could more easily see the signs, but he became increasingly abusive against my mother." Out of the corner of my eye, I saw Saylor flinch and turn away. At that moment, I became more worried about her than how hard this story was to tell. I turned in my seat and took her hand. "Look at me, sweetheart."

Her cheeks were flushed, and while she looked at me, she had a hard time maintaining eye contact.

"He never laid a hand on me. I suppose because he saw in my eyes what would happen if he did." I took a deep breath, willing myself to continue the story I hadn't told anyone for years. "I came home one night and saw his car in the driveway. I can't explain the feeling that came over me, but I knew something was going to happen that night that would change me for the rest of my life."

I met Saylor's gaze. "Are you okay?"

"Yes. Go on."

"I could hear yelling, so instead of going in the front door of the house, I went around to the back. As I came up the back porch, I could see him. He had a baseball bat and was about to hit her."

"What did you do?" Saylor asked.

"I killed him," I said with every finality I felt that night. "It was her or him."

"What happened to you?"

"Nothing. Surprisingly. Not even manslaughter. The cops knew the history of our family. They also knew his record. It was determined to be self-defense almost immediately."

"You did what you had to do, Monk."

"My father was the first man I killed, Saylor. There have been others."

"It's part of what you do. Just like it's part of what Razor does."

"Not everyone can accept it."

"Before you left, I told you I believe the decisions you make are the best ones given the circumstances of the situation you're in. Is there truly anyone you've killed that you regretted later?"

I thought it over for a minute. There really hadn't been anyone. Like with my father, it was a matter of protecting the innocent from the evil.

"Were you afraid I would think less of you, Monk?" Saylor shook her head and looked away. "Believe me, I'm in no position to judge."

"I don't tell everyone that story. It isn't everyone's business, but I had to tell you."

"Can we go back to the house now, Monk? I don't like being so far away from you."

I nodded. I could reach out and touch her, and she could do the same, but it was nothing like skin-on-skin. I put the Jeep in gear and backed out of the parking area. As we drove back to Saylor's place, a feeling of dread settled over me. It wasn't about her reaction. She understood the decision I'd made that night.

This was something different. I had no idea what was coming, but whatever it was, wouldn't be good.

18

"Hi, Aine. What brings you over?" I asked when Ava's sister knocked on my open door. "Come on in."

"Do you know Stuart Anderson?"

"The plumber?" I regretted my question the second I asked it. I'd known Stuart most of my life, and he wasn't just a plumber. "I'm sorry. Yes, I know Stuart."

I felt even worse when Aine's cheeks flushed a bright red.

"We've gone out on a couple of dates."

"That's great," I said, trying my hardest to recover from my previous gaffe but fearing I sounded insincere.

"I think Razor totally intimidates him. I was wondering if maybe you and Monk might like to go to dinner with us sometime."

If Razor intimidated Stuart, I doubted Monk would make the man feel more comfortable. Heads didn't turn when my brother walked into a room. Well, women's heads turned, but in a way that said they wanted to get to know him better. Monk, on the other hand, seemed to attract attention wherever he went. While he was oblivious to it, I noticed it from the first time he found Poppy and me at the bar in town.

"I think that's a great idea. I'll run it by Monk and get back to you."

"Thanks," Aine answered, looking everywhere but at me.

"Look, I'm sorry if I came across badly. It's just that everyone kind of knows he's a plumber."

"It isn't that."

"Have a seat, girlfriend, and tell me what it is, then."

"You know I was seeing Striker last year."

I'd wondered about that. They'd seemed hot and heavy, and then there was nothing.

"He and Stuart are very different."

"I may be overstepping here, but the spy life isn't as glamorous as some people think it is. Razor is still my irritating little brother who's always been so full of himself that I'm surprised his neck still holds his big head. Don't get me wrong, I love him, but the truth is, for many years, he was gone more than he was home. I think your sister changed that, but that doesn't mean they'll all change. Every one of them—Monk, Striker,

Gunner, my brother—they all chose the life they lead. I'm sure they get off on the danger as much as they tell themselves it's their calling."

Whoa. Where had that come from? My subconscious talking much? Who was I talking to—myself or Aine?

"Thanks, Saylor. I needed to hear that."

"Anytime."

A week later, Monk and I went to dinner in town with Aine and Stuart. As I expected, Stuart didn't seem the slightest bit comfortable. In fact, he seemed a lot angrier than the guy I'd known most of my life. I hoped that at some point Monk and Aine might leave the table at the same time so I could ask Stuart what the hell was up his ass. I didn't get the chance, and it was probably better that way.

"What did you think of Stuart?" I asked Monk on the way home.

"Something's off there."

I rested my head against the back of the seat. I agreed, but I couldn't put my finger on what it was.

"What's bothering you?" he asked.

"Nothing's wrong," I answered, but not truthfully. The conversation I'd had with Aine a few days ago repeated in my head. I'd warned her that not all of the K19 team members would prioritize a relationship over their career—not that I wanted one. I stifled a groan and turned my head so he couldn't see the look on my face.

"Don't lie to me, Saylor."

"Wait a minute. What did you just say?" He wasn't wrong, but I bristled at him calling me out on it.

"I can't do anything about it if you won't tell me what's on your mind."

"What it is, is nothing, like I said."

He nodded and focused on the road ahead of us.

"I've got a long day tomorrow," he said after he'd pulled the Jeep into the garage and I hopped out without waiting for him to come around the other side.

I had a long day tomorrow too. In fact, I had a lot of time to make up for. Since Monk waltzed back into my life, I'd slacked off on flying. Time on the ground was adding up faster than time in the air, and I needed far more of the latter than the former.

"Good night, Monk," I said when he climbed on the motorcycle and was about to put on his helmet.

When he started the bike, I went inside. As soon as I heard he was gone, I'd come back out and close the garage.

When I returned a couple of minutes later, the garage was already closed and Monk and his bike were gone. Did that mean he somehow knew the code for the keypad that was outside the door? The fact that he might, pissed me off more than the fact that he hadn't even bothered to try to kiss me goodnight.

"What's wrong?" Razor asked when I was getting ready to leave for the airfield the next morning.

"What are you doing here?"

"I came over to tell you that Cliff has a parole hearing coming up."

"When?"

"Next month."

"When next month?" I snapped.

"It isn't important. I'll take care of it like I always do." Razor turned to walk away.

"Then, why even tell me?"

"I don't know. I won't make that mistake again."

My brother walked down the trail back to his house, leaving me with a boulder in the pit of my stomach. What was wrong with me? Monk had asked me the same thing last night, and Razor had before he'd even said good morning. Obviously, I was throwing off some powerful vibes I wasn't aware of. Maybe after my flight today I'd see if Poppy had some time to get together.

That was another thing. Why did I only think about calling her when something was wrong?

—Monk—

I looked up from the computer when Razor walked in and slammed something down on the desk.

"Sorry," the man muttered.

A few minutes later, he did the same thing, followed by a slew of obscenities.

"Everything okay, boss?"

"No, it isn't."

"You wanna talk about it?"

Razor pulled out the chair next to me, spun it around, and sat on it backwards. "Did something happen with you and Saylor?"

This was absolutely not a conversation I intended to have with anyone but her, especially not with her brother.

"That isn't any of your business."

"The hell it isn't. I haven't seen my sister like this since…before."

I knew what Razor meant, so I threw him a bone. "No, nothing happened with us, but I sensed something is wrong."

"Maybe she knew about the parole hearing before I told her, but she didn't act like she did. She isn't the kind of person who *acts* any way. She just is who she is."

"Parole hearing?"

"Her ex. It's scheduled for next month. I'm working on getting a delay, but there's only so much I can do."

"Can I help?"

"How?"

"Don't ask questions you don't want the answers to."

Razor studied me for a minute. "Is it legal?"

"Like I said…"

A few minutes passed without Razor saying anything. Finally, he stood and pushed the chair up to the desk. "Do it," he said as he walked out of the office.

It only took me a few minutes to hack into the Oregon judicial system and get the hearing pushed back six months. That was standard; if I'd gone for any longer, it would've raised suspicion. As the next hearing date got closer, I could do the same thing again.

I turned back to the monitor I'd been watching before, studying the movements of Abdul Ghafor, a man who should be dead if not imprisoned for the rest of his miserable life. Instead, he'd been able to secure a deal with the CIA, who had given him exile in Columbia, South America.

Granted, Ghafor's information led to the impeachment of a standing US president, who had been convicted of election fraud on a massive scale, along with several others who had aided in that fraud. The fact that Ghafor had been part of that ring himself meant he had the proof the CIA needed to take the entire operation and each of its players down. And thus, he wrote his own exile ticket.

Ghafor hadn't been in Columbia long when K19 heard chatter that led us on the hunt to see what he was up to. Sure enough, Abdul had returned to Pakistan and was now stockpiling enough weaponry to stage an attack on a gargantuan level.

But where? That was the reason K19 hadn't swept in and annihilated him already. First, we needed to know a whole helluva lot more, including who was funding the weapon stockpiling, who his supplier was—which could be one and the same—and finally, what he planned on doing with it all. An attack on US soil was most likely, but why would Ghafor gnaw off the hand that gave him a get-out-jail-free pass?

It was my job to monitor who came and went, and while I could clearly see the faces of the men who periodically delivered the truckloads of weapons, none of them appeared on K19's or the US's radar. I had each of them scanned into facial recognition and placed on every alert system I could, but so far, there hadn't been any hits.

Later today, I would head to the airfield to pick up Striker Ellis, Diesel Jacks, and Ranger Messick. Striker was the lead on this op, given he was the authority on South American covert activity with the CIA while employed by them and still, now that he wasn't.

Doc Butler had called a meeting of the entire K19 team, which would be taking place here in Yachats. While a general meeting like this took place bi-annually, I knew Ghafor would be the primary focus of this one.

I was on my way to pick up the K19 team members when I noticed a familiar-looking Jeep in the airfield's parking lot. There was no question it belonged to Saylor. She hadn't mentioned anything the night before about going on a trip or about needing to be at the airfield, although something was definitely off with her. Even Razor had noticed it.

When I left with my three passengers in the car, I took a second look at the parking lot, and the Jeep was gone.

When I got back to Razor's place, it didn't look like she was home either.

"Moving on, our next topic of discussion should raise the heat level in the room—Abdul Ghafor," said Doc after we finished the introductory portion of the partner meeting.

"We've confirmed he's in Pakistan and that he's stockpiling weapons," said Razor.

"What about soldiers?" Doc asked.

"That's the thing. There's very little sign of feet on the ground."

"Weapons mean money," I said.

"Shit," said Razor, clutching his chest. "Raise your damn hand or something when you do that."

"What?"

"Talk."

I flipped him off.

"Striker? Fill us in," said Doc, sitting down next to Merrigan. "Where's the money coming from?"

"I'd say that's obvious."

Doc motioned for Striker to stand.

"Look, it's no secret that I vehemently disagreed with the CIA's decision to exile Ghafor to Colombia. I have little doubt that the money is coming directly from the Islamic fundamentalists who have taken a stronghold in Buenaventura."

"Led by whom?" asked Merrigan.

"They're doing a damn good job keeping that a secret."

Razor had his laptop open and was scratching his chin. "Let's reopen dialogue with the Cuban."

Striker nodded.

From what I could remember, sometime last year, a Cuban national had been arrested in Bogotá for an alleged "terror plot" to kill American diplomats on behalf of Islamic State extremists. The plan had been for the man to blow himself up inside a restaurant popular with US Embassy staff and other foreigners in the *Zona Rosa* region of the city. K19 had played an integral role in neutralizing him before he could put his plan in action.

"Is he still alive?" asked Razor, staring at his computer screen.

"To the best of my knowledge, although I doubt for long. Colombian officials amassed a trove of evidence against him," answered Striker.

"It's your mission, Ellis. What do you do?" asked Doc.

"Hypothetically?"

"Not necessarily."

Striker put his hands on the table in front of him. "What I'd want to do is assassinate the bastard. However, in doing so, I'd lose the money trail along with his connections to the terror plot in Bogotá, as well as the lesser-knowns."

"First phase, then?" asked Razor.

"We watch. Concurrently, we get someone on the money."

"Eighty-eight is damn good at tracking financials," Razor said. Mercer, or Eighty-eight as Razor had called him, was renowned for his forensic accounting abilities.

"You mentioned at the beginning of this meeting that Mercer would join us for phase two of the mission we would be discussing. Is this the mission?" asked Striker.

"Affirmative," answered Doc.

"What's phase one?" Striker asked.

"That's up to you, to a certain extent anyway. Let's nail down the basics. While Razor has a badass new setup here, the logistics of keeping everyone in Oregon are a nightmare. Therefore, I propose we work out of what is quickly becoming K19's Central Coast headquarters."

"Back to phase one," said Razor, looking at Striker.

"We watch, and we'll know when to make a move."

"Roger that." Razor stood, picked up his computer, and walked over to where Striker was seated. "We're teaming up on this one," he said. "But it's your mission. I'm number two."

"Who's on our team?" Striker asked.

"Your call, but for the time being, I say we put everyone on standby. Between the two of us, Monk, and Eighty-eight, we can handle surveillance. If anything changes, it's easy enough to call in the cavalry."

"Agreed." Striker looked at me. "You're number four."

"Copy that," I responded.

19

"I don't understand. Everyone will be there," my mother told me over a week later when she came over to ask why I wasn't going to Cambria for Thanksgiving.

"I'd rather spend a quiet day with the girls instead. I've been so busy flying that I feel like I haven't done that."

"Bullshit."

"Excuse me?"

"You heard me. I said 'bullshit.'"

"Mom, I don't—"

"I'll tell you what I think."

"I didn't ask," I mumbled.

"I'm telling you anyway. You got scared. Monk got too close, and instead of handling it like an adult, you retreated."

"You're out of line, Mom."

"Everyone else may be afraid to call you out, but I'm not. I've never spent a holiday away from my grandchildren, and I don't plan on doing it this year."

"Then, stay here."

"I have other grandchildren, young lady."

I hung my head. My mother was right. About everything. I'd done more than my share of soul-searching since Monk left the other night, and while I vacillated between beating myself up a little versus a lot, the bottom line was, I was ashamed of the way I'd acted.

"I'm leaving in the morning, and I expect you and the girls to go with me."

"Okay," I muttered.

"I'm sorry, I didn't hear you."

"I said that the girls and I will go with you."

"Good." My mother turned and stalked out of my side of the house. I didn't remember her ever getting as mad at me as she did today. My brother, yes, but not me.

When we landed the next morning, I received a text from Razor saying there'd be a black SUV waiting outside the airport terminal to transport us from the San Luis Obispo airport to Cambria. He didn't say who would be driving it.

When we walked into the baggage claim area, I got my answer. Sierra and Savannah saw Monk first and raced over to him. I loved that he knelt down to hug each of them, but his eyes stayed focused on mine.

"Hi," I said, walking closer to them.

Monk released the girls. "Let me say hello to your mama."

When he stood, I walked into his arms. "I'm so sorry, Monk."

"Shh," he whispered, stroking my hair. He put his fingers on my chin and raised it. "Is the no-PDA rule still in effect?"

I shook my head.

"Good." He captured my lips with his, thrusting his tongue in my mouth. I didn't care if it bothered my daughters or anyone else in the airport. I needed to feel his mouth on mine. Needed to feel his body next to me.

"I missed you so much," I said when he ended our kiss and rested his forehead against mine.

"I missed you more."

I grinned. Every so often, he said something that was so un-Monk-like that it took me by surprise.

"Let's get your bags."

I turned and saw they were already on the baggage carousel and Sierra and Savannah were both running alongside them.

"I'll do that," he said when Sierra tried to grab one.

I stood back and watched as his powerful arms flexed when he lifted the bags off. I didn't have to close my eyes to picture exactly how he'd look without clothes covering his perfect body. The image heated my core; I couldn't wait to be alone with him.

I looked up from studying his rock-hard ass, and realized he was looking right at me. And smiling.

"Where are we staying?" I asked as he led us to the waiting vehicle.

"Your mother and the girls are staying with your brother and Ava. You and I are staying at a place on Moonstone Beach."

"You reserved a room? For us?"

Monk nodded.

"What if…"

"You didn't come?"

It was my turn to nod.

"I didn't consider that as a possibility."

"We haven't talked recently."

My mom and the girls got in the SUV while Monk loaded the luggage. Instead of getting in myself, I hung back with him. He closed the doors to the rear cargo area and put his hand on my nape, drawing my lips to his. He kissed me more deeply than when we were in the airport.

"We don't always need to speak to know."

I laughed. "We don't? I have to admit, I'm not as clairvoyant as you are."

"The night at the bar, when I showed up unannounced on my motorcycle. How did I find you?"

"I figured you saw my car."

Monk shook his head. "And later that night, when you got in your car, why didn't you drive away?"

"I was crying too hard."

"No. You didn't leave, because you knew this wasn't finished between us. You got scared, you tried to run, but you couldn't. Just like I can't."

He kissed me again and looked into my eyes. "I'm going to say something that is going to scare the ever-living shit out of you, Saylor."

"Okay."

"You and me. We're meant to be together, and we will be. No matter what, we'll find our way back to each other."

"How can you be so sure?"

Holding me against him with one arm, he brought the opposite hand to his heart. "Because this is where

I feel you. Every day." He kissed me one more time before walking me to the front passenger door.

"There's something else I need to tell you."

"Okay," I repeated.

"This op is heating up. There's a chance I'll have to leave without much warning."

Part of me wanted to tell Monk that he didn't need to explain. I understood. But that was at the heart of what had been bothering me before and still bothered me now. It was one thing when it was my brother and he was doing his job. Of course I'd worried about him, particularly after he'd ended up on life support. It was different with Monk. I worried about him in a different way, and if I was really being honest, I didn't like the fact that he had to be gone so much. I'd never tell him that, but it was how I felt.

"Saylor?"

"I heard you."

"This is hard for you."

"It's hard for everyone."

He cupped my cheek with his hand and looked into my eyes. "I'd promise you that I'll be back, but I can't do that. All I can tell you is that I'll do everything I can to make sure that happens."

My eyes filled with tears. "I know."

"Saylor, I—"

I put my fingers on his lips. "It's okay, Monk. I truly do understand."

"You don't know what I was going to say."

"Yes. Actually, I do."

I opened the door and climbed inside.

—Monk—

"I heard back from the Bogotá consulate. Your meeting with the Cuban is set," Razor said to Striker while I continued tracking Ghafor's movement.

"When?"

"As soon as you can make arrangements to leave."

"Where's Onyx?"

"On standby," I answered. I knew because I'd just gotten off the phone with him.

"We're meeting at eighteen hundred hours," Striker said when he ended the call.

"Got a minute?" asked Mercer, looking between all three of us and then laying out several documents on the table.

"What have you pieced together?" Razor asked.

"The Islamic fundamentalists in Buenaventura, Columbia, have done a good job covering their tracks to this point. There is no history of money transfers. However, today I found out why."

Mercer pointed to several of the transactions on the printouts. "Without monitoring the activity every day, we would've missed these. The transactions are purged at the close of business."

Striker shook his head. "There's no end to what Ghafor could do with this kind of money."

Mercer looked directly at Striker. "We have to stop him. I don't think we can afford to wait any longer."

"I agree," I said, even though no one had asked my opinion.

"Do we act before or after Bogotá?" Razor again directed the question at Striker.

"After. It's likely the last chance we'll have to find out who's running the show in Buenaventura."

"Roger that," said Razor, returning to the monitors with me. "Any leads yet?" he asked Mercer.

"Not yet, but catching the money was the first step. Now that I have, I can start tracing it."

"Got a minute?" Striker asked me.

What the fuck else did I have to do that was more important than this? "Yes."

"It can't be as simple as the Colombian fundamentalists supplying the Islamic State leader with the kind of money Mercer's talking about. They'd never be able to raise as much cash as has been transferred today, not to mention how many other days similar amounts have been moved."

I agreed. More likely, the money was coming from someone with much deeper pockets. There were two possibilities. First, one of the drug cartels was supplying the money. Second, any country that considered the United States an enemy, and there were too many of those to count. It could be anywhere from Venezuela to Russia.

"Who's going with you to Bogotá?" Mercer came into the hallway and asked.

"Ranger and Diesel, along with Onyx and Corazón in the cockpit."

"Get in and out as quickly as you can," said Mercer. "I don't have a good feeling about this."

"Fuck," said Razor, ending a call on his phone. "Juan Carlos is dead."

The Cuban Striker was on his way to meet with. "Any other intel?" I asked.

Razor shook his head. "Jiménez told him personally."

"Did they meet?"

"They are now. He's got Ranger and Diesel with him to do reconnaissance."

"What about Onyx and Corazón?"

"Still with the plane."

I turned back to the monitors. There was something about Corazón that didn't sit right with me. I hadn't spent a lot of time with her when I stayed on the plane with her and Onyx, but it didn't take a lot of time to get a bad feeling about someone.

I turned back around to face Razor, glad no one else was downstairs with us. "How well do you know Descanso?"

"Not well."

"She vetted okay?"

Razor walked over and sat beside me. "Talk to me, Monk."

I told Razor my opinion of her. "I can't say it's anything specific."

"It doesn't need to be," Razor responded. "If anyone rubs you wrong, don't ever hesitate to say something, Monk. It's what keeps us alive."

"Roger that."

"Let's get through this op, and in the meantime, I'll run some more background on her."

"Look at this," I said to Razor, pointing at the screen. "They're moving the arms." I indicated another monitor. "And look where our friend Abdul is."

"Ghafor is back in Columbia?"

"Affirmative."

When Razor left, I made sure the monitors were recording properly and went upstairs. I hadn't slept in forty-eight hours. I hadn't spent time with Saylor; I barely knew what day it was. As much as I wanted to crawl into bed with her, I knew I needed sleep more.

20

—Saylor—

"Hey," I said when I saw Monk coming up the stairs. I walked over and put my arms around his waist. "You have to take a break, Monk."

"I know I do."

"Have you slept at all?"

"Negative."

"Wait here. Don't go anywhere." The man was dead on his feet. Where would he go?

I found my mom next door, talking to Gunner's mother. "Can you keep your eye on the girls for a little bit?"

"Of course," she answered, standing. "Where are they?"

"Next door."

"I'll walk back with you and bring them over here."

I kissed her cheek. "Monk needs some rest. I'm going to let him sleep in your room."

"That's fine, sweetheart."

I thanked my mother again and then rushed back over to make sure Monk was still waiting for me. He was, thankfully.

"Come with me," I said, taking his hand and leading him over to the stairs. I held his hand as we walked down the hallway and opened the door to the bedroom.

"Go lie down, Monk," I said, closing the blinds. By the time I lay next to him, he was sound asleep.

I wrapped my body around him anyway. All that mattered was feeling him next to me. The last couple of days had been so hard. I knew whatever K19 was in the middle of, was something serious enough that it drew everyone here, and yet we rarely saw any of the team members. Razor came up more than anyone else, but it was his house. Every time he did, he immediately went to find Ava and Sam. As much as I wanted to ask about Monk, I didn't. I knew better.

I must've drifted off, but woke when I felt Monk stir beside me.

"I need to get back," he muttered.

I looked at my watch. "You haven't even slept four hours, Monk."

"I'm sorry, Saylor." He brought his lips to mine.

"You don't have to say you're sorry to me. I'm just worried about you."

He kissed me again and brought both of his hands to my breasts. "I want you so bad I can't stand it."

I pushed him back on the bed, unfastened his belt, and unzipped his pants. Before he could protest, I kissed him.

"Let me do this." I trailed my lips down the front of his shirt and wrapped my mouth around his hardness.

—Monk—

"Where in the hell have you been?" asked Striker when I walked into the downstairs office. Doc, Mercer, and Gunner were there too, and all of them were looking at me as though they expected an answer.

I pushed past them and sat in the chair next to Mercer. "What's this about?" I asked.

"Monk," said Striker. "I asked you a question. Where have you been?"

"Sleeping," I responded without turning around.

"Rhys."

I spun around and looked at Doc, who said, "Onyx filed a flight plan earlier today. We aren't certain of the details, but it appears that he, Corazón, Tackle, and Halo are on their way to Colombia."

I turned to Striker. "I thought I was the handler on this."

"There he is," said Razor, walking into the office, breathless.

"Anybody wanna tell me what the fuck is going on?" I asked.

Mercer stood, and Striker sat down in his place.

"Did you authorize their deployment?"

"Whose?"

"Jesus Christ, Monk! Onyx, Corazón, Tackle, and Halo!"

"You said to put them on standby, and that's what I did." *What the fuck was going on?* "Has anybody made contact with Onyx?" I asked.

"Negative," Mercer answered.

"How'd you find out about the flight plan?" Gunner asked no one in particular.

Everyone else in the room looked at Razor.

"I got a call from Jiménez asking if Striker was on his way. I asked what he was talking about, and he responded that there was a K19 plane in the air."

"What did you tell him?" asked Doc.

"That his intel was bad."

"Meaning what exactly?"

"There was no K19 plane I knew of on its way to Colombia."

"What did he say?"

"He told me it was *my* intel that was bad."

"Has anyone actually confirmed the plane is even in the air?" asked Gunner.

I looked around the room; everyone was staring at me. If what we were dealing with wasn't so serious, I'd get up and walk out. How dare they question me. I'd been in this goddamn room for the last two days. "I hadn't slept in forty-eight fucking hours," I muttered.

"Why didn't you tell anyone you were leaving?" Razor asked.

"Seriously?"

He stared me down.

"The last I checked, I was a partner in this fucking firm, and I don't ask permission." I stood to leave, but Doc put his hand on my arm.

"Monk, you're right. What we need to figure out now is whether there is a plane en route to Colombia. Once we've confirmed there is, we need to figure out who authorized its departure."

"I'll ask again, has anyone made contact with Yáñez?" I spat.

"Negative," answered Razor like Mercer had in his absence. "I've attempted contact with all four we believe are on board—Onyx, Corazón, Tackle, and Halo. No response."

"You *believe* to be on board? Have you seen the flight plan? What about the manifest?"

"Negative. There wasn't time," Razor answered.

"How long since you spoke to Jiménez?" Striker asked Razor, who checked his phone.

"Thirteen-ten," he answered.

"It's thirteen-thirty-five now," said Striker. "My answer, Monk, is we've been trying to figure this out in real time. We need your help."

I picked up my phone.

"Gentlemen," said Razor, motioning for everyone to leave the room. "I can't believe I'm saying this, but we have several women upstairs who have been cooking for the last few days in order to serve a large group of people Thanksgiving dinner."

"Understood. We'll eat in shifts," answered Doc. "I'll head up and speak with Merrigan. Striker, who do you want to stay down here with you and Monk?"

"I'll stay." Mercer volunteered.

While they were all worried about eating fucking turkey, I was trying to figure out why the hell Onyx would've gotten in the air without my okay. Something was seriously wrong, and it was making me sick to my stomach.

I pulled up the flight's manifest. "Fuck."

Striker sat down next to me. "What?"

"It's all here. Flight plan, manifest, departure log."

"Out of Miami?"

"Atlanta."

"Where are they now?" Striker asked.

"That's the thing," I said, shaking my head. "They're nowhere."

"Come again?"

I pointed first to one monitor and then the other. "That's the last flight segment before they went silent. This is a hundred-mile radius." I motioned with my head to the other two monitors. "These are five hundred and one thousand miles."

"Have you made contact with Venezuelan air traffic?" Striker asked.

"I'm doing that now," Mercer answered.

"I'm going to ping Razor."

I nodded; that was a good idea.

"Get everyone back down here," Striker said when Razor came rushing in.

"Roger that," he said, turning around.

"The Venezuelan power grid is completely shut down," said Mercer when the rest of the team gathered in the office.

"What do you mean?" asked Gunner.

"The entire country is dark," I answered.

"That's impossible."

I put on my headset and held up my hand, signaling everyone to stay quiet so I could hear the broadcast coming out of Venezuela. "It's not. President Maduro just announced a state of emergency. Get the feed," I said to Striker.

"Here it is," he said, turning the monitor's volume up.

We listened as the country's current president accused José Guaidós, the US-backed incoming leader of Venezuela, of sabotaging the power grid.

"They have one fucking grid," muttered Gunner, shaking his head.

Razor rubbed the back of his neck. "It doesn't explain why we lost contact, or why the plane isn't showing up on the radar. Neither would be affected by one country's grid."

"It would if they were diverting and/or blocking signals," I responded.

"What about Jiménez?" asked Doc.

"My gut is telling me to leave the ambassador out of this," answered Striker.

"I agree," said Doc.

"Anything?" Striker asked me; I shook my head.

"Is anyone thinking the same thing I am?" said Razor, cutting through the uncomfortable silence.

Doc rubbed the back of his neck with his hand like Razor had. "Four of our teammates are on a plane that was last seen in Venezuelan airspace. We know their government isn't going to do a damn thing to help us find it. We can't do this alone. We need to contact the agency."

"If we think this plane is down, I'm going in," said Striker, looking first at me and then at everyone else in the room.

"I am too," said Razor. "Who's with us?"

My hand went up as did every other hand in the room.

Striker sat down next to me. "You tell me. What should we do?"

"Best if we split into teams. One to Bogotá and one closer to where the plane lost contact."

"Flying into Maracaibo would make the most sense, but would it even be possible with the power grid down?" Striker asked.

I shook my head. "The closest we can get is Aruba."

"Cope can arrange for aircraft and pilots," Doc said after ending his call with the CIA handler.

I studied the screen. *Fuck.* As if this could get any worse. Now, there was a goddamn hurricane showing up on the region's radar. "No one is going anywhere until tomorrow at the earliest," I said, pointing to a different radar report on the monitor.

While it was late in the season and both Aruba and Colombia were below the hurricane belt, in order to get to either, we'd have to fly directly through the eye of an impending storm.

Not only would it ground us, but it would make any search for the aircraft and its occupants exponentially more difficult.

"It's Cope," said Doc, looking at his phone. He walked into the hallway to take the call.

"Where's the fucking plane?" muttered Striker.

"Tabon?" I heard Ava call out from the stairwell.

"Monk, is there anything else we can do right now?"

I shook my head.

"Go eat, then."

I didn't acknowledge Razor had said anything to me.

"He means you," said Striker.

I turned and looked into Striker's eyes. "I need quiet to do this."

Striker motioned for everyone to head out. "I'll be back in a few minutes."

"I'll let you know if I need you."

Nausea overwhelmed me once everyone left the room. Why in the hell had Onyx filed that flight plan after I specifically told him to stand down until he received further word?

No one else on the team had given him authorization. If they had, I would ream their ass for it. I closed my eyes, trying to piece together a possible explanation. I saw one face: *Corazón.* She had something to do with this; I could feel it in my bones.

21

It broke every cardinal rule, but I went looking for my brother regardless. Something was going on, and whatever it was, felt as serious as when he'd been shot. He could refuse to tell me, but I had to ask anyway.

I found him in the kitchen, carving more turkey.

"Can you take a minute?" I asked.

Razor set the carving knife and fork down and ushered me out into the garage.

"Not a word to anyone," he warned.

"Understood."

"We've been dealing with something in South America. There was a K19 team on standby to fly in when we believed it was necessary. We don't understand why yet, but that plane took off without authorization from any of us. Monk is the handler on this op, so it's hitting him pretty hard."

"Why? Because they took off without his orders?"

Razor shook his head. "The plane has disappeared. We believe it went down."

I covered my mouth with my hand. "I told him he needed sleep…"

Razor pulled me into his arms. "This isn't any more your fault than it is his. And you were right; he hadn't slept in two days, which meant he was a liability to the op. He knew that, which is why he took the break to begin with."

"How is he?"

"Wrecked. We all are."

"What's next?"

"We're making arrangements to leave now."

"Thank you for telling me, Raze."

"He's down there alone. Go talk to him, Saylor."

"Are you sure I should?"

"He needs you."

I followed my brother back into the house and then went straight downstairs. The door was open, and I could see Monk looking at computer monitors, but I knocked anyway.

"Saylor," he said, turning around and holding out his hand.

"Razor told me to come down. He told me about the plane."

Monk pulled me onto his lap and rested his head against mine. I could feel his body shake and the dampness of his tears on my shirt.

"I'm so sorry," I whispered.

Monk held me tighter, but didn't say anything.

He raised his head and spun around with me still in his lap when the monitors started beeping loudly.

"Go get your brother," he said. "Tell him we got a ping."

"From the plane?"

"Yes. Go!"

I ran up the stairs and found Razor where he'd been before in the kitchen.

"Monk said to tell you he got a ping."

Razor dropped the knife and fork, and ran from the kitchen.

—Monk—

"Where is it?" Razor shouted as he ran into the office.

"Coordinates indicate Macuira National Park. There's a team headed there now, but with the storm, I don't know if they'll be able to reach it."

"Any audio?"

"Negative. Let Striker know."

Razor left the room.

This was Striker's op, but there was no way in hell I would leave this room myself to give him the update. If anything at all came through from the plane, I didn't want to miss it.

"Anything?" Razor asked when he came back downstairs.

"DEA have the coordinates of the plane. No one has gotten close yet due to the storm combined with the terrain," I answered.

When Striker, Doc, and Mercer came in, Razor reiterated what I'd said.

"How soon can Cope arrange transport?" Striker asked Doc.

"Do we know if we can even fly yet? What's the status of the hurricane?" Razor asked.

"Planes and crew are on standby at LAX. I've been told they're cleared to fly." Doc looked at me.

"That's correct."

"There's a CH-53K out of Vandenberg that can get us to LAX in under an hour," added Mercer.

"Get as much of your gear together as you can from here," said Doc, motioning to the closet that held enough full tactical gear for the entire team. "I'll give

Merrigan an inventory of whatever else we need while we're on the road to the airfield. She'll make arrangements to have it delivered to the plane in Los Angeles," Doc added.

"You mean planes, right, Doc?" asked Gunner.

"Affirmative. We'll split into two groups. Striker, who do you want with you?"

"Me," said Razor.

"And me," I said.

"Gunner, Mercer, and I will be team two," said Doc.

"What about Ranger and Diesel?" Razor asked Striker, who looked at Doc.

"Let me see what Cope can do. What's their twenty?" Doc asked me.

"Right outside DC."

"I want to run something by you," Razor said to Striker and me once we were on the plane that would take us to Colombia.

"Shoot," said Striker.

"I have an idea as to why Ghafor is stockpiling weapons, or for who—FARC."

Striker nodded and I agreed. Especially given the tentative peace agreement the Marquez-led Colombian government and the Revolutionary Armed Forces of Colombia, aka FARC, that came into effect in 2016 was already falling apart.

The treaty had been historic in that it had taken fifty years to bring the conflict to an end, but the implementation of the accord was beyond optimistic. The government and FARC weren't the only two entities vying for power in Colombia—the drug cartels had more power than each of the two on their own, but less if they joined forces.

No matter who was involved—politicians, insurgents, or drug barons—corruption was rampant. Not to mention the Islamic fundamentalists who had settled in Buenaventura. The entire country was a ticking time bomb.

"At least we know what we're dealing with when it comes to FARC, the government, and even the cartels. For me, the big unknown is the Islamics," said Striker.

"What's your take on Jiménez?" Razor asked.

"Don't trust him," I answered.

"Yeah? What's your take, Monk?"

"Think about it. Jiménez agrees to meet with Striker; Juan Carlos is killed between the time you leave the

States and arrive in Colombia; Ghafor moves the arms, and the peace treaty falls apart."

"Who do you think is orchestrating this?"

"One of the cartels makes the most sense," Striker said to Razor.

"Keep going."

"Which one has Jiménez in their pocket?"

"All of them. There are no good guys," I muttered. "We should let 'em annihilate each other."

"If only," said Striker. "What about the plane? You think this is a coincidence, Monk?"

"Fuck no. Somebody set us up."

"Any idea who?"

"How'd you find out the plane was in the air?" I asked Razor.

"Jiménez contacted me."

"Exactly. Here's my question—how the hell did anyone know that I was the handler on the op? Someone like Jiménez could've assumed you were the lead, but why would Onyx pull the trigger on the flight plan without checking in with me first?"

"You didn't hear a word from him?" asked Striker.

"You don't think that's the first place I went? Not a fucking word."

"I heard you were on board," I heard a man who had just walked onto the plane say to Striker. "How the heck are you, Ellis?"

"You know Razor Sharp and Monk Perrin. Boys, this is Trap Flannery. We go way back to my first day at the agency."

"We haven't met although I've heard of both of you."

I nodded in response but didn't say anything. I looked beyond the two men, relieved when I saw Mantis and Dutch board the plane.

"Hello, boys," said Mantis, shaking everyone's hands.

"Heard some of ours are MIA," Dutch said to me before turning to Striker. "Can't believe you didn't call me."

"Heard you were retired."

The minute the plane landed in Columbia, Striker's, Razor's, and my phones started blowing up.

"I'll call Cope," said Striker, putting the call on speaker.

"DEA agents found the plane," the man said.

"*And?*" Striker shouted.

My head shot up.

"I'm waiting for confirmation as to the specifics, but the word I received was there were three critically injured and one fatality," Cope told him.

"Goddammit," Striker swore. "Where are they?"

"As you know, the plane was found in Macuira National Park. Because of the situation in Venezuela, the survivors were airlifted to the university hospital in Magdalena. I've made arrangements for a private aircraft to take you to Simón Bolívar International Airport where a car will take you directly to the hospital."

"Who's the fatality, Cope?" Striker asked, making eye contact with me.

"I'm sorry, Striker. I don't have confirmation on that yet."

"Who knows about this?"

"Which part?"

Striker rolled his eyes. "The next leg of our trip."

"Right now, you, me, the owner of the plane, Mantis, and Trap. He'll make the rest of the arrangements as soon as you've deplaned."

"Tell me, Cope, do the DEA agents think the crash was accidental?"

"Not sure yet, but there's a crew headed to the wreckage to investigate."

"Where's the black box?"

"With the DEA until the investigators arrive."

"How soon until we head out?"

"Like I said, Trap is making the arrangements."

"What about the rest of our team?"

"Working on transport for Doc, Gunner, and Eighty-eight now."

"Ranger and Diesel?"

"In the air. We'll make that determination after you arrive at the hospital."

"Thanks, Cope. If you hear anything about the condition of our team, contact me immediately."

"Roger that, and, Striker, Godspeed."

"Hey, wait. Who's the plane's owner?"

Cope hesitated. "I can't tell you that, but I need you to trust me."

"I don't get it," said Razor. "Why won't he tell us whose plane we're flying out on?"

I turned and saw Trap headed toward us. I jumped up and stalked over to him, slamming him up against the wall of the cabin. *Whose plane is it? Tell me right fucking now.*"

"Franz Lehrer's."

I released the pilot and shoved him away. "We're taking a fucking Armenian-born drug baron's plane? In what universe would anyone agree to this?"

"The one where the CIA is working with him to take down the Cali Cartel, FARC, and Petro Santos."

Striker shook his head, muttering my thoughts exactly. *"Jesus Christ."*

What this meant was the FARC combatants and the Colombian government weren't falling apart after all. Instead, they were working together, along with Mao's Cali Cartel, to ensure an end to Latin America's oldest and most stable democracy.

"What about Ghafor and the weapons?" I asked.

"Buenaventura is in Medellín-controlled territory."

"Ghafor's working with the CIA," said Striker.

"You didn't really think we were that stupid, did you, Striker?" said Trap.

"Not all of you." Striker made no secret that he had zero respect for Money McTiernan, who had orchestrated Ghafor's supposed exile.

I didn't agree with him. My experience was that Money knew a fuck of a lot more than he ever let on.

"Don't underestimate McTiernan," said Trap, like Striker reiterating my thoughts. "You didn't suspect a thing."

"Who supplied the weapons?" Striker asked.

Trap looked at me.

That was obvious. "United fucking Russia," I responded.

Striker believed the CIA gave Ghafor free rein. I didn't agree with that assessment either. I'd known Money and the rest of the powers that be had something up their sleeve. I just hadn't known what.

What I couldn't see past, though, was that because the CIA didn't read us in on it, our plane had crashed and someone on board died. If we'd known what we were walking into, there was no way in hell Onyx would've put that plane in the air without my direct authorization.

I listened as Striker walked us through his summation.

The CIA put Ghafor exactly where they wanted him and gave him a specific mission—to help them get rid of Santos, put Marquez back in power, and save the crumbling democracy before it was too late.

The money, which I guessed came from the CIA, flowed through the Medellín Cartel, to the Islamic

State, to UR, who then supplied the weapons—believing the endgame was to reinforce Santos' power.

Instead, Ghafor made arrangements to have the arms shipped to Colombia. With that kind of firepower, Franz and the Islamic State would have the combined ability to take down the Santos administration as well as FARC, and thus, put the CIA's man back in office.

If word of this got out, that the company collaborated with one of the largest drug cartels in Colombia, it might bring the agency itself down. The US had recently lost one president due to one of the biggest conspiracies in the nation's history. The one K19 found ourselves in the middle of was almost as big.

"How high up does this go, Trap?"

"I can't answer that."

Striker looked as angry as I had a few minutes ago. "Three of our team are critically injured. One is dead. I want to know who's responsible."

Trap shook his head. "I'm sorry, Striker."

"Why was our plane in the air in the first place? No one from K19 authorized Onyx's flight plan. No one pulled the trigger on that part of the mission. I want to know who did, when, and why."

When Trap shook his head again, Striker pushed past him and got off the plane. A few minutes later, he came back and got right in Trap's face.

"Someone on that plane was in on this. Who was it? Tell me *right fucking now*."

"Corazón."

"Who was she working for?"

"Santos."

I sat down when Striker did. If I hadn't, my legs would've given out. Razor walked over and put his hand on my shoulder.

"I gave you specific orders to finish out the op. This isn't on you, Monk."

"The fuck it isn't. I knew she was dirty. Knew it." What I left unsaid was that because I'd followed orders, there was a chance either Onyx, Tackle, or Halo were dead. Unless she was the one who'd died, the minute I had the opportunity, I'd kill Corazón with my bare fucking hands.

Trap and Striker were still talking about her, but I tuned them out. When I heard Striker say, "She was the fatality," my head shot up.

"Affirmative," said Trap. "We believe she was able to convince Onyx that they had the go-ahead to deploy."

Onyx must've somehow figured out Corazón was intercepting the messages and then knew she'd lied to him. Maybe he even realized she was working for the other side. My guess was that once Corazón realized he was onto her, she'd tried to kill him. Or vice versa. We wouldn't know the whole story until Onyx was able to tell it.

"I'm having a hard time wrapping my head around this," said Dutch. "Corazón and Onyx were tight."

"The rest of your team has arrived," said Trap, looking out the window.

Before anyone could stop me, I stalked out onto the tarmac. When Doc got off the plane, I walked up to him.

"Corazón is dead. She was the double agent."

Doc looked into my eyes but didn't say anything.

"I need to go in and get Onyx out of there. Not just him. Tackle and Halo too. Don't fight me on this, Doc."

Like Razor had, the man put his hand on my shoulder. "Name your team, and before you say anything, I'm your second."

"Mantis and Dutch."

"You got it."

22

—Saylor—

"Oh my God," I said when Razor came to my house a few days later to tell me everything that had happened.

"Monk is in Columbia now with Doc, and they're arranging to bring Onyx, Tackle, and Halo back to the States."

"Is it safe for Onyx to travel?" Razor had said he was in a coma and in the ICU at the hospital in Magdalena.

"We have a team of doctors and nurses flying back with us. It's his only chance, Saylor. We can't leave him there."

"How is Monk?"

"The last time you asked me that, I told you he was wrecked."

"And now?"

"It's a hundred times worse."

"What can I do, Raze?"

"When I figure that out, I'll let you know."

"If you talk to him, tell him…"

"I'll tell him the truth."

My eyes met my brother's.

"If there was ever a time he needed to know that you love him, it's now, sis. And don't even try to tell me you don't."

"We haven't said those words to each other."

"Like I said."

"Okay."

"You understand you can't tell anyone else what I've told you. Not even Mom."

"I do, and I want you to know how much I appreciate you trusting me."

"Like I said, you're in love with Monk. You deserve to know what's going on in his life." Razor winked and stood. "Oh, we thought it might be a good idea to spend Christmas in Annapolis again this year. That way, we won't be far from DC."

I cocked my head.

"We're taking the boys to George Washington University Hospital."

Christmas was still a couple of weeks off. Hopefully, I'd be able to talk to Monk between now and then to confirm that's where he'd be. If Razor was going to tell the man I loved him, I wanted to see him in person to affirm it myself.

—Monk—

I hadn't left the ICU since we arrived at the hospital. After seeing Razor right after he'd gotten out of a coma, it was hard to imagine that Onyx ever would. The man's extremities were all in casts, and he had tubes in his nose and mouth. Very little of his face even showed between those and the bandages covering his head.

It had taken a few tries, but eventually, I understood what the nurse was trying to get across to me in broken English.

"Him. Talk," she said again and again.

I wondered how the hell Onyx was supposed to be able to talk with all the fucking tubes in his mouth. Finally, I realized she was telling me to talk. What she didn't understand was that was equally impossible.

I couldn't think of a single thing to say, so I just sat there until the nurse told me to take a break. When I went out into the waiting room, Doc was sitting alone, looking at a magazine.

"That in English?" I asked.

He shook his head. "I'm looking at the pictures." He turned the magazine around so I could see the scantily clad Latino woman on the page. It reminded me of the time Onyx and I were in Brazil and two women who looked like they were decked out in Vegas showgirl attire had approached us on the street. They wanted five hundred reals, or about one hundred US dollars to allow Onyx and me to take a photo with them. Granted, neither of us had asked. I shook my head and laughed.

"What?" asked Doc.

"Just remembering something that happened when I was on an op with Onyx."

Doc scrunched his eyes. "I take it, it's a funny story."

"Yep," I said, knowing exactly what I was going to do once the nurses let me back in to see Onyx.

Once I got started, I thought of countless stories to tell Onyx. I had so many that I started writing down reminders when I thought of them. I didn't limit them to things that had happened between just the two of us; there were plenty of other things that had happened with other agents, even with civilians, that I could tell him about. I even told him about playing the pig game with Saylor's daughters and how they kept insisting I shriek "*Soooooie*."

"Everything is ready," Doc said the next time I came out of the ICU. "Once we get our men on the plane, we can go home."

"I know you hate being a passenger, dude, but just this once, you gotta," I said, leaning over my friend so I was close to Onyx's ear.

"You're a good man, Monk," said Doc when we walked out of the ICU behind the gurney carrying our teammate.

I shook my head and pointed in front of us. "That's a good man right there."

23

I walked over to turn up the volume on the television. "Shh."

"What?" asked Poppy, looking at the screen. "Since when do you give a shit about South American politics?"

I held up my hand and listened to the reporter say that Colombia's president, Petro Santos, had been assassinated. He also reported that the man had recently been linked to the Cali drug cartel.

Carlos "Mao" Deodar, leader of that cartel, had also been assassinated on the same day. While he was killed in a different part of Colombia, it was believed the two deaths were related.

An emergency election was being called, in which former President Juan Marquez was predicted to be re-elected. If so, it was expected that he'd take office immediately and restore normalcy to the embattled nation.

Razor had come over a second time to tell me that Onyx was still in a coma but believed to be stable enough to be transported to the States. That was ten days ago, but I hadn't heard a word from Monk in that time.

Tomorrow, the girls, my mom, and I would be leaving for the East Coast to spend Christmas at Gunner's family's home in Annapolis, like we had the year before.

"I take it the news about Columbia has something to do with Monk," said Poppy, motioning to the TV.

"Indirectly, but yes."

"Have you heard from him?"

I shook my head.

"Did you try calling him?"

I hadn't, and I didn't intend to. I needed to see him face-to-face, and that's what I planned to do.

—Monk—

"You gotta take a break," said Striker, coming in to find me by Onyx's bedside, reading a book aloud. "It's fucking Christmas, man. Onyx's family is here. If not them, let some of us take over, even if it's only for a few days."

"Never been big on holidays."

"This isn't your responsibility."

I stood up so fast the chair I'd been sitting in toppled over. "Get the fuck outta here," I seethed.

"Hold on a minute. This was my op, Monk. You feel guilty? Guess what? So do I."

I motioned Striker out of the room and followed him. If what the docs and nurses had told me about Onyx being able to hear us talking was true, I didn't want him hearing what Striker and I were fighting about.

"It isn't the same—"

"It's exactly the same. In fact, if anyone should be here day and night, it's me, not you."

"It isn't your call."

Striker sighed. "I know it isn't, Monk. I'm trying to give you a break. Let me."

"I didn't ask for one."

"*Jesus,*" Striker muttered. "How about this? Why don't you come to the house for Christmas at least, so you don't spend it alone."

"You think the man fighting for his life in that room should spend it alone instead?"

"He isn't alone, Monk. His family is here."

"Fuck off, Striker." I turned around and went back inside, hoping Striker would take the hint and leave.

Evidently, he had, because the next people I saw, two hours later, were Tackle and Halo.

I'd known both Landry "Tackle" Sorenson and Knox "Halo" Clarkson since their CIA days. Which, for the two of them, wasn't that long ago. Both men had suffered minor injuries when the plane crashed, nothing as severe as Onyx's.

When the two men were getting ready to leave after being there over an hour, I offered to walk them out.

"I'm sure you've already briefed Doc about this, but what went down that day?"

Tackle rubbed the back of his neck with his hand. "It was a major Charlie Foxtrot, Monk."

"I don't know what went on in the cockpit before that, but when we were almost to Aruba, all hell broke loose." Halo closed his eyes, and when he opened them, I wished I hadn't asked either of them to relive such a traumatic event.

"We heard a shot fired and stormed the front of the plane. It all happened so fast. Onyx had taken a direct hit and Corazón was turning her gun our way when I fired," said Halo.

Close range for both shots. The one that hit Onyx and the one that hit Corazón. It's a fucking miracle the man was still alive. Not only had he survived a plane crash, but he'd taken a direct hit too.

"By that time, the plane was already taking a dive. I didn't think there was any way we'd live through it," said Tackle.

"I'll tell you what, every day since we've been home, I've told as many people as I can that I love them. Even my aunts and uncles, who probably think I've lost my mind," said Halo. "I don't care. The other thing is, life is too fucking short to not have someone you love by your side. I know that isn't easy to find, but when I do, I'm gonna make damn sure I don't waste any time."

"I feel the same way," said Tackle. "Any time I find myself thinking I'll put something off until the next day, I stop and do whatever it is right then. I came too damn close to not having any more next days."

I'd asked; they hadn't offered, but it felt as though every word they were saying was meant specifically for me to hear, and it ripped me up.

I loved Saylor; I knew I did. I wanted to spend my life with her and her two beautiful girls, but I couldn't ask them to let me. What kind of life would it be with me gone all the time? The girls needed someone who was home every night, who could tuck them into bed, help with their homework, and make their mama smile. Even if I could bring myself to ask to be a permanent part of their lives, how in the hell would that work? What would I do, ask them to move to Washington, DC?

I shook my head at my own thoughts. Until Onyx could walk out of this hospital by my side, I wasn't going anywhere.

24

"Do you want me to go with?" Razor asked as I was putting on my jacket.

I put my hand on my brother's cheek. "No, but I appreciate the offer."

"At least let me drive you. The weather's shit."

"There's no way I'm taking you away from Ava and Sam on Christmas, Razor."

"We already celebrated. Now, we're just hanging out."

I shook my head. "I doubt your wife would see it that way. Christmas dinner hasn't been served yet."

"Okay, but remember I offered." Razor opened the front door.

"What's that supposed to mean?"

He pointed to the SUV sitting in the driveway as a man I didn't recognize climbed out to open my door. "Your ride, sis."

"I'm perfectly—"

"Let me do this so I don't worry and ruin Christmas dinner."

"You're so full of shit." I stood on my tiptoes and kissed Razor's cheek. "But I love you anyway."

"Tell Monk we all said hi."

I would if I saw him. I still wasn't sure I would. And even if I did, maybe it wouldn't be for long. After all, I still hadn't heard from him and today was Christmas.

I had to try, though. At least to tell him how I felt and that whenever he was ready, I'd be waiting for him. Even if it took forever. The vow I made to never fall in love again was back in place. This time, though, I knew I'd never fall in love again after Monk.

With the lack of traffic, it only took the driver forty-five minutes to get me to the hospital. As we pulled up to the front entrance, I almost told him I'd changed my mind and asked him to take me back to Maryland, but when I looked up, I could see Monk walking toward the door.

"Thanks," I shouted, jumping out and half running, half walking inside. I pulled my phone out of my pocket.

Look up, I wrote and hit send on the text. He did.

"Hi," I said as we walked toward each other.

"Saylor."

"Merry Christmas, Monk."

"What are you doing here?"

"My mom, the girls, and I are spending Christmas in Annapolis again this year. How's Onyx?"

"No change."

"I'm sorry, Monk. I was praying for a Christmas miracle."

I watched as he took his one glove off and put both of them in his pocket. I looked into his eyes when he took another step forward. He gripped the back of my neck with one hand, wrapped his other arm around my waist, and kissed me. If there was anything I would've asked for as a Christmas gift, this was it—a kiss from Monk.

He pulled back and looked in my eyes. "I'm sorry—"

I put my fingertips on his lips. "Don't. Where were you going?"

"Dinner."

I tucked my arm in his. "Good. I'm hungry."

"It's cold," he said as we left the hospital.

"I'm okay to walk." I snuggled against him, praying I wasn't dreaming. How many times had I dreamed we were together again? Countless.

"This is nice," I said when we exited the elevator in his building and he opened the door to his loft.

I walked around, looking in the opened doors. "It's big."

I turned around when I didn't hear him respond and saw he was looking inside the refrigerator. I walked over and wrapped my arms around his waist. "When did you last eat?" I asked.

"Lunch. You said you were hungry."

"I can wait."

Monk closed the refrigerator door and led me into the master bedroom.

I watched him undress, like I always did. He unbuttoned his white dress shirt, revealing so much that I didn't know where to look first.

"Is this new?" I asked, running my finger over the black beads intricately wound with leather.

"It is."

"For Onyx?"

"Yes."

As he eased the shirt off his arms and shoulders, I unfastened the heavy copper buckle on his jeans.

He grasped my small wrist in his big hand. "Wait, Saylor. We need to talk."

"Okay," I said, backing up to sit on the end of the bed.

He knelt in front of me, taking each of my hands in his, turning them over, and kissing my palms. "There are some things I need to say to you, Saylor." He looked into my eyes. "I need you to let me finish. Even if you think you don't want to hear it, you have to promise to let me finish."

My eyes filled with tears.

"First, I'm sorry. I should've called you, and I have no excuse for not doing so. I'll tell you this, though; I think about you every day. As I sit in that hospital and watch machines keep a very dear friend of mine alive, I think about you. This might surprise you, as it did me, but I spend most of my day talking to Onyx."

"Out loud?" I asked, smiling.

"Yes, out loud." Monk leaned forward and kissed the tip of my nose. "I tell him stories about you and me and the girls, and sometimes I just talk to him about how I feel about you. Most importantly, though, is that no matter where I am or what I'm doing, you're there with me. When I sit in a restaurant alone, I close my eyes and imagine you're sitting across from me. When I leave the hospital at night, I get off the elevator and imagine what it would be like to find you there, waiting for me."

"Like tonight."

"I was sure I was dreaming." He put his hands on the hem of my sweater and pulled it over my head. He tossed it on the floor and then reached around to unfasten my bra. He slowly slid it off my arms and took a deep breath when my breasts were exposed.

"I dream of having my mouth on you," he said before his lips encased my nipple. "God, I want you." He rested his head on my lap. "But I have so much more to say."

I wove my fingers in his hair that had gotten so long.

He sat back on his haunches and looked into my eyes. "Your brother gave me a message."

I opened my mouth to speak, but he shook his head. I lowered my gaze.

"Look into my eyes, Saylor."

I couldn't bring myself to do as he asked. Was I ready for this?

"Look at me."

I couldn't deny him when he used the demanding tone of voice.

"I love you."

I closed my eyes briefly, took a deep breath, and then opened them. "I love you, Monk."

We both ignored the sound of a ringing cell phone that came from the other room, until the tone changed.

"That's the hospital," said Monk, standing. "I'm sorry, but I have to get it."

—Monk—

"Perrin," I answered.

"Mr. Perrin, Mr. Yáñez's family asked us to contact you."

I held my breath. It was Christmas. Had Onyx really given up his fight for life on the holiest of holidays?

"Mr. Yáñez is awake, sir. They wanted us to let you know right away."

My eyes opened wider. "Please repeat what you just said."

"Mr. Yáñez is awake. He's also communicative. This is a direct quote, sir. He said, 'Where is that bastard Monk who's been talking my ears off?'"

I reached around Saylor, standing next to me, and pulled her body close to mine.

"Sir, the family asked if you would come back to the hospital."

My eyes met Saylor's, and she nodded.

"I'll be right there." I ended the call but didn't move. "Is this real?"

Saylor pinched my side. "Did you feel that?"

"Do it again. Harder."

She giggled.

"Yeah, I felt it."

"It's real, Monk. It's a Christmas miracle."

"Onyx's family has asked that I come back to the hospital. I know it's late. I hate to leave—"

"I'm going with you."

"Right. Okay." I looked around the apartment. What did I need to do before we left? How long might we be gone? "You haven't eaten."

"That's what hospital cafeterias are for. Although right now, I'm too excited to eat."

I raised a brow, and Saylor swatted my stomach.

"Excited that Onyx is awake."

I was smiling. In fact, I was smiling so much my face was beginning to ache. How long had it been since

I really smiled? Sometimes I laughed when I told Onyx one of my stories, but the laughter ended quickly when I stopped and prayed that one day soon, my friend would laugh with me.

"They said he asked for me."

"Of course he did. Let's go see him."

I cupped her cheek with my palm. "Thank you, baby, for understanding."

Saylor told me she'd wait outside the ICU, but I dragged her with me.

"He's heard more about you in the last few weeks than anything or anyone else."

"I don't want to be intrusive."

I refused to let go of her hand. Our visit would be brief anyway. Not only had the man just come out of a coma, but his entire family was in town. The ICU only allowed two visitors at a time. I'd go in, talk to my friend for a few minutes, and then we'd head back to my loft.

When we exited the elevator and the door opened, Onyx's mother ran to me before I could step out.

"Es un milagro," she exclaimed, tears running down her cheeks. "My son, he asks for you," she said

in a thick Hispanic accent. When the elevator doors closed with me still standing in the threshold, Onyx's mother let go, and I stepped around her.

"This is Saylor," I said, taking her hand.

"Sí, you've spoken of her often." She gave me a shove. "Go now."

I walked past Onyx's brothers and sisters, nodding at each of them as I went. They all looked so happy.

When I eased the door open to the room where I'd spent countless hours, Onyx opened his eyes.

"What, did you go back to sleep?"

"Being awake is exhausting." Onyx looked past me. "Is that Saylor with you?"

I put my hand on the small of her back.

"It's so good to see you," she said, walking closer to his bed. "Merry Christmas."

"Merry Christmas, and it's good to be seen." He reached out his hand to her. "He's talked about you nonstop," he said, motioning to me.

"Yeah?"

"He told me to hurry and wake the fuck up so he could go home."

"Nice." I shook my head.

"Tell her it isn't true," said Onyx.

"She knows it is."

He motioned for me to get closer, and when I did, he grasped my hand. "You kept me alive, son."

"You did that all on your own. And, by the way, I'm older than you are."

Onyx smiled. "In age maybe, but certainly not in wisdom."

I smiled back, and my eyes filled with tears. I'd prayed endlessly for this—to hear my friend's voice giving me shit like he always did.

"We should go. Let some of your family get back in here."

Onyx refused to loosen his grasp on my hand. "You are my family. You're my brother. Even if you are a pain in the ass."

"I'll be back in the morning."

Onyx shook his head. "Take the day off, son. You've earned it."

I shook my head as well.

"I'll instruct the nurses not to let you in."

"They won't listen. They like me."

Onyx chuckled. "Give me an hour, and they'll like me better."

No doubt, I thought. Onyx never had any trouble charming the ladies. I took a deep breath. Soon, we'd have to talk about one lady in particular—Sofia "Corazón" Descanso—and what the hell had happened in the hours that led up to the plane crash. There'd be time for that, though.

"Keep him in bed all day tomorrow," Onyx said to Saylor, winking.

"It would be my pleasure," she answered, winking back.

I shook my head and gave Onyx's hand one more squeeze. "I'll see you soon."

"I have a feeling I'll be here a while."

"As will I."

25

—Saylor—

Monk waited until the next morning to call Doc and tell him the news. While they talked, I called Razor and filled him in.

"Words can't describe my relief, sis."

"I get it, Raze. I really do. You should come down and see him."

"Can he have visitors?"

Monk ended his call, so I asked him.

"I would think so. Doc and Merrigan are flying in later today."

"On what plane?" Razor asked, laughing. "I think all the K19 planes are on the East Coast." My brother cleared his throat. "You got a minute alone?" he asked.

"Of course." I went into the other room.

"We're going to need a co-pilot on the way back."

"Yeah?"

"You up for it?"

"Wait. What? Me? Are you serious?"

"Why are you whispering?"

Honestly, I couldn't say. For some reason, I still hadn't told Monk about getting my pilot's license, and other than the fact that there hadn't been time, I had no explanation.

"When?" I asked instead of answering Razor's question.

"We were talking about tomorrow, but with Onyx coming around, we'll probably stay a few more days."

If they were still leaving tomorrow, I would've been torn. I wasn't ready to leave Monk yet, even to take K19 up on their offer to let me be in the cockpit on the transcontinental flight.

To think, my first gig as a commercial pilot would be to transport not only K19 team members back to the West Coast, but my mom and girls too. It was almost too much to wrap my head around.

"Everything okay?" Monk asked when I came back inside.

"Yes, fine."

"Saylor?"

I looked up at him.

"Are you sure everything's fine?"

"Yes. Of course." I walked over and put my arms around his waist. "Onyx is awake. What could be better?"

—Monk—

As Onyx had told her last night, I had every intention of letting Saylor keep me in bed all day. We'd gotten up to eat and so I could call Doc and let him know the good news. Our plan had always been to get right back under the sheets and continue ravishing each other's bodies. Something was wrong though, and whatever it was, Saylor was unwilling to share it with me.

I hated secrets, but maybe for now, it was best to hold back whatever it was she didn't want to talk about.

"As much as I hate to say this, I need to leave tomorrow," she said three days later.

I had been expecting it. The girls would have to get back for school, and the rest of the crew based on the West Coast needed to return to their lives. I wished I could go with them, but I was committed to stay and help Onyx with his recovery and rehabilitation.

"You don't have to do this, son," Onyx had said to me the night before when Saylor and I were leaving for the night.

"It isn't up for discussion," I'd said.

"I don't know when I'll be able to leave, Saylor," I said now.

"I'm not asking, Monk. It isn't that I don't want you to come back to Yachats with me tomorrow, but I respect your commitment to helping Onyx."

"Thank you for coming. I mean that sincerely."

She smiled like she always did. God, this woman. She made my heart do somersaults. We hadn't said "I love you" since the first night, but we showed each other with our bodies.

"I'll take you back to Annapolis in the morning."

"That's okay. Razor said they'd pick me up on the way to the airfield."

"I'm going to miss you."

"I'll miss you too, Monk."

Our lovemaking that night felt more like goodbye forever than it did "see you soon." As much as I tried to shake off that feeling, it only intensified.

26

—Saylor—

"Nervous?" my brother asked when we arrived on the tarmac.

"To a certain extent. Knowing there's one pilot in the cockpit with me and another in the cabin in case I really fuck up helps."

Razor laughed and rubbed my shoulders. "You're gonna do great, like you do with everything."

"You have to say that; you're my little brother. And I'm not great with everything. There are things I supremely suck at—like relationships."

I looked over at my two girls. Being their mother was the most important part of my life. Did having a man around really matter in the long run? My mother hadn't looked at another man twice since Razor's and my father died.

"Didn't you just spend a few days with Monk? Is there something I'm missing?"

"Our lives are so different. I'm not sure we have any chance of succeeding in the long term."

"What happened? Last I saw, you were all lovey-dovey. Do I need to go hurt him?"

I looked around to make sure no one appeared to be eavesdropping. "He doesn't know anything about me getting my pilot's license."

Razor raised a brow. "Why not?"

I shrugged. "I can't explain it. At first, I wasn't ready to tell anyone, in case I failed. Now, I'd have to explain why I've gotten this far without telling him."

"This isn't like you, sis."

"I know."

"Ready?" asked Mantis, motioning toward the plane.

"As I'll ever be."

"You should be a flight instructor," I told him fifteen minutes later, after he'd walked me through various system checks.

"I've done a lot of training in my lifetime. On both sides."

"You're good at it."

"Let's see you repeat everything I just showed you."

I went through the same series of checks Mantis had and then waited.

"Perfect. What's next?"

I went through what I'd do next in a smaller aircraft. "You're a natural," he said, smiling.

Mantis stayed engaged throughout the flight, letting me figure out certain things on my own, pointing out what I missed, and praising what I did right.

It almost seemed too soon for us to begin our descent; the flight seemed to have gone so quickly.

Once we'd landed, I was giddy. Especially when my girls came running up to me, asking a million questions all at once about what it was like to fly the plane.

"I didn't fly the plane, Mr. Gehring did."

"Don't let her be humble," Mantis said, kneeling down so he was on their level. "Your mama did a fantastic job getting us home safely."

I had to admit, few things felt better than seeing the look of awe and pride on my daughters' faces.

"We'll be back in the air at zero eight hundred tomorrow," Mantis said. "Get a good night's sleep."

"What do you mean?"

"We're transporting Doc and Merrigan to DC tomorrow."

"Are you saying that I'm going?"

"Hasn't Doc talked to you?"

"No. He hasn't."

"Well, my bad, then. I know he intends to, though. With Onyx and Alegria both grounded and…" Mantis lowered his voice. "It isn't like Corazón was around that long anyway. My point is that Doc is anxious to get you on the payroll."

I was too stunned to speak. Never in a million years would I have guessed that learning to fly would result in getting a job offer.

"I never…"

"What did you never?" asked Razor. "Did Mantis tell you Doc wants to open a dialogue about bringing you on board?"

"Is he serious?" I could tell he wanted to make a smart-ass remark, like both of us were prone to. Instead, he got emotional.

"I'm so fucking proud of you, Saylor."

"Thanks, Raze. But the girls…"

"Will get to spend more time with their Ya-Ya." My mom had tears in her eyes. "I'm proud of you too, sweetheart."

As good as it felt to have my family's support, it would've been so much better if I could call Monk and give him the news. But I couldn't, because I hadn't been brave enough to share my dreams with him. Since we were flying back to the East Coast, maybe I'd have time to see him. If I did, I'd tell him all of it and hope he understood better than I did why it took me so long.

—*Monk*—

Onyx had been moved to a room on the rehab floor, which meant the number of visitors he could receive at a time had doubled. The nurses, however, reminded us that a hospital was no place for the party that was currently taking place.

"Too bad Saylor isn't here to toast with us, but Mantis was anxious to get back," said Merrigan, clinking her glass of sparkling wine to mine.

"What do you mean?"

"I think she was hoping they'd have a layover."

I looked from Merrigan to Doc, who appeared to be following our conversation. When I walked out to the hallway, Doc followed.

"What's she talking about?"

"We've offered Saylor a permanent pilot slot as soon as she completes her final commercial test."

I leaned back against the wall. "She didn't say anything."

"We didn't talk to her until this morning. I know Mantis mentioned it to her yesterday, but maybe she wanted to wait until she knew for sure," said Merrigan, who had joined us.

I pushed off the wall. "I gotta go." Rather than wait for the elevator, I looked for the stairwell, ran down the nine flights of stairs, and stalked out the hospital's front entrance. I walked by my building and kept going. Nothing about the conversation I had with Doc and Merrigan made any sense. When in the hell had Saylor become a pilot?

I'd been walking over an hour when I found a park bench under a tree. I pulled my phone out but just stared at the screen. If I called, what would I say? I sure as hell couldn't send her a text. Plus, didn't Doc say she was already flying back to the West Coast?

The sick feeling in my stomach got worse. Before I put my phone back in my pocket, I turned it off.

27

"You're way overthinking this," said Poppy. "He'll be thrilled for you."

"I'm not so sure."

"No offense to either of you, but it isn't like either of you communicate very well."

I glared at her. "That isn't fair."

"It isn't? The man comes back from butt-fuck Egypt and doesn't bother to get in touch with you when he does, even to say he's planted himself at his comatose friend's bedside, and by the way, Merry fucking Christmas." Poppy shook her head. "You aren't any better. Did you call him? Hell, no. You just 'understood.' Well, you shouldn't have understood."

"Are you finished?" I asked, folding my arms.

"No. There was a reason you didn't tell him. Think about that for a minute."

"I haven't stopped thinking about it."

"I don't know Monk very well, because he never talks, but how does that even work? Do you know anything about his life?"

"He's told me things he never told anyone else."

"Okay, let's say that's true."

"Are you serious? Why would I lie?"

"I don't know, Saylor. Why would you?"

"I think you should leave."

"The hell I will. Ask yourself this. Is this because of Cliff?"

I shook my head and walked into the kitchen.

"Is it?"

"I don't know what you're talking about."

"Is Monk the kind of guy who wouldn't want you to have a life of your own? Would he have told you not to become a pilot like Cliff did?"

"No, but Cliff didn't either."

"Right. You were pregnant, and then a year later, pregnant again, and then a mom. But you're still a mom, Saylor, and you made it happen. You wanna know what I think?"

"You haven't started telling me yet?"

Poppy shook her head. "You two deserve each other." My friend grabbed her bag along with the packet of unpopped popcorn that she'd brought with her and stalked out of the house. I jumped when she slammed the front door behind her.

I'd checked my phone every minute for the last two hours, waiting for some kind of word back from Monk. I'd called him shortly after Poppy left, and when the call went straight to voicemail, I left a message asking him to call me as soon as he could. "I have a lot to tell you," I said before ending the call.

Two hours wasn't a long time, but I wouldn't be able to shake my feeling of dread until I was able to talk to him. I'd decided I was going to be as honest with him as possible and tell him I couldn't explain why I hadn't told him what I was doing until now.

Since I couldn't concentrate enough to do anything including cook, I took Sierra and Savannah to a local pizza place. When they begged me to stop on the way home so they could see Aunt Ava and their cousin, I did.

"Are you okay?" Ava asked after we'd been there a half hour.

"I'm fine. Why?"

"You've looked at your phone about once a minute since you got here."

"I'm sorry," I muttered, putting it in my back pocket.

"Don't apologize. Tell me what's going on."

"I'm waiting to hear back from Monk."

"Do you know where he is?" Razor asked.

My eyes scrunched. "At the hospital?"

"Nope. Doc said he took off a few hours ago, and they haven't heard from him since."

"Is he required to be there every minute?"

Razor sat down next to me. "Doc also said that he and Merrigan let the pilot cat out of the bag."

My cheeks flushed, my skin felt like there were a thousand prickles trying to break through from the inside out, and I was sure I was about to be sick to my stomach. I couldn't even look at my brother or sister-in-law, especially when my eyes filled with tears.

"I'll go check on Sam and the girls," said Ava, leaving Razor and me alone.

"You okay?"

"Do you really think the two are related?" I asked.

"You do."

I did. Razor was right.

—Monk—

It was dark by the time I got off the bench and began the walk back to somewhere. I hadn't decided yet where I'd go. I didn't want to go to the hospital, but that wouldn't be as bad as going to my loft where everywhere I looked, I'd see the memory of Saylor.

I powered on my phone and saw missed calls from both Doc and Saylor. I thought about turning it back off or deleting the message she left, but I did neither. Instead, I listened.

"Hi, Monk. Can you call me when you get this? I have a lot to tell you."

I stopped at the liquor store on the way to my loft and bought a bottle of Hennessey. Once home, I poured some over ice and sat down on the sofa, turning my phone over in my hand.

28

"Hi," I said, answering Monk's call.

"Saylor."

"How are you?"

"What did you want to tell me?"

"I know you already know this, but I've spent the last few months getting my pilot's license."

"Yeah?"

"My brother said Doc told you they made me an offer to come to work for K19."

"Yes."

I didn't know what else to say. It felt like I was talking to a stranger—someone I'd just struck up a conversation with, who knew nothing about me and was responding just to be polite.

"How's Onyx?"

"Not much different than he was two days ago."

Okay, then. This conversation was going nowhere.

"Thanks for returning my call, Monk."

"Take care, Saylor."

I stared at the phone's screen. *Call ended,* it said. Ended. Over.

"I love you too, Monk," I said out loud before turning my phone off and putting it in my pocket.

"That sounds like it went well."

"Yeah, it was great, Raze."

I walked into the bedroom where my daughters were lying on the floor, playing with my nephew, who looked like he was getting fussy.

"Time to go, girls."

Thankfully, neither argued.

I managed to get them home, baths done, looked over their homework, and read them a bedtime story. Once I was sure both were asleep, I sat in the quiet until I fell asleep in their room too. I woke sometime in the middle of the night with a sore neck but a worse ache in my heart.

Once in bed, I couldn't go back to sleep. My mind turned my conversation with Monk over and over. Each time, it ended the same way.

When the alarm went off, I was still awake. I got up and made the girls' lunches before going in to wake them. Once I was sure they wouldn't go back to sleep,

I went back into the kitchen and made them pancakes. I drew smiling faces with syrup and poured them each a glass of milk.

"Are you okay, Mama?" Sierra, always first to be ready for school, asked when she climbed up on the kitchen counter stool.

"I'm more than okay," I said, leaning forward and kissing her cheek. "I have some big news, but we'll wait until your sister's here to talk about it."

"What news?" asked Savannah, climbing up to sit next to her sister. Both started firing questions at me.

"Is Mr. Monk coming back?"

"Is he going to live with us, Mama?"

"Will he be our new daddy?"

"Are you getting married?"

"Can we be flower girls even though we're your daughters?"

"Stop!" I shouted, immediately regretting my tone. "Look, my news has nothing to do with Mr. Monk."

"Oh," muttered Sierra. Savannah took a bite of her pancakes.

I attempted my best fake smile. "I got a job offer."

"What's a job offer?" asked Savannah.

"It's when someone wants you to work for them, dork," said Sierra.

"Hey, now," I scolded. "That kind of talk isn't necessary."

Both girls stared at me.

"Are you finished?"

They went back to eating.

"I'm going to be flying airplanes for Uncle Razor's company."

When neither girl responded, I threw up my hands and dug into my own pancake.

"Who's picking us up from school today?" Sierra asked when we got in the car to leave for school.

"I am."

Sierra looked at Savannah, and neither appeared happy about it.

"Have a good day. See you later," I said once we got to the front of the car line. "I love you," I added, but the car door had already closed behind them.

I went back to the house and thought about trying to pull the dead plants from my neglected garden, but I was crying too hard to see what I was doing. Instead, I sat in the grass, lowered my head, and let the tears flow.

When I felt a man's hand on my back, I knew it was my brother's. I wished so much that it was Monk's instead.

"What happened?" Razor asked, sitting down next to me.

"He hung up on me."

"When?"

"You walked into the kitchen and heard me say I loved him too. He'd already hung up. And he didn't say it first."

"Come here." Razor put his arm around my shoulders and pulled me close to him. "I never liked him anyway," he said, making me laugh.

"I wish I felt that way." I wiped my nose on my sleeve and then brushed away my tears. "I swore I'd never do this again."

"Cry? Good plan."

I laughed again. "Let a man wreck me."

"Better plan."

"What is wrong with me, Raze?"

"Not a damn thing."

"I'm being serious."

"So am I. This isn't on you, Saylor. Monk is weird as fuck. I mean, I know you like him or love him or whatever, but even you have to admit he's a strange dude."

"He really isn't. He just doesn't talk when there's nothing to say."

"See? Who does that?"

—Monk—

Onyx wasn't in his room when I got there the next morning, and I didn't bother finding out where he was. Instead, I pulled the chair over by the window and looked out at the gray sky. I leaned forward, put my elbows on my knees, and let my head drop.

"You look like shit, son."

I looked up and saw Onyx being wheeled back into the room. "So do you."

"I was in a plane crash. What's your excuse?"

"Where you been?"

"Physical therapy," he said, trying to lift himself out of the chair.

"You gotta wait, man," said the orderly, shaking his head. He looked over at me. "Can you give me a hand?"

I got up and walked closer to the wheelchair.

"I can do it," spat Onyx.

"You were in a plane wreck, remember?" I followed the lead of the orderly and put my arm under Onyx's and lifted him onto the bed. It was obvious he had no control over his legs, and when our eyes met, I saw his fear.

Once Onyx was settled, I walked back over to the window.

"You can take off," Onyx muttered.

"I'm not going anywhere."

"Getting tired of seeing your mug around here."

I shook my head and pulled the chair closer to the bed. "Tell me what the doctors are saying."

It took Onyx a long time to answer, but since I had nothing else to do, I waited.

"Just because my eyes are open doesn't mean the rest of my brain has woken up yet."

"Knew that before the plane crashed. What about your legs? When are they gonna wake up?"

I caught the grin on Onyx's face that came and went too quickly.

"Don't fuckin' know."

"What's the rehab setup like?"

"First-rate. Better than the damn food."

"Hear ya there." I stood. "What do you want?"

"Is this how it's gonna go, Monk? You're gonna be my nursemaid?"

"You see anybody else here?"

"Thank you."

"You're welcome. Now, what do you want to eat?"

29

—Saylor—
Four Months Later

"Thank you so much for helping me set all this up," said Ava, while I tied ribbons to the last of the balloons for Aine and Striker's baby shower. "I can't believe my sister is having twins."

"They run in the family, don't they?"

"Yes, but I thought they skipped a generation."

"Guess you were wrong. You aren't, are you?" I pointed to Ava's quickly expanding belly.

"You sound like your brother. Although less panicked."

I laughed.

"How are you?" she asked, resting her hand on my arm.

"Really good. Busy flying and then reminding Sierra and Savannah that Ya-Ya's rules only work in her house and, in my house, they have to eat with their mouths closed. I swear if I'd pulled the shit my mother lets them get away with, I would've had bruises on the backs of my hands from getting hit with a fork."

"Really?" Ava's eyes were as big as saucers.

"I think the threat of the fork was enough for Razor and me to mind our manners."

"Have you talked to Monk?"

"Nope," I answered, a little too quickly and definitively.

"What happened between you two? If you don't mind me asking."

"Nothing. His base is on the East Coast, mine is on the West."

"Simple as that," Ava said, raising an eyebrow.

"Leave it alone, Avarie."

I turned and looked at my brother. It was unlike him to even frown at his wife, let alone be so abrupt with her.

"What's going on?" I asked when Ava stormed out of the kitchen.

"News about Cliff."

"He's getting out, isn't he?"

"I'm sorry. There was only so much I could do, Saylor."

"It isn't your responsibility to keep him in prison, Raze."

"I would if I could."

"Maybe he's rehabilitated."

"Men who strike women aren't capable of rehabilitating." Razor's eyes met mine. "I'm sorry, maybe I shouldn't have said that."

"You're worried."

"Honestly, I am."

"What should I do?"

"Live your life."

"Who are you putting on our detail?"

Razor grinned. "Smarty-pants."

"Who, Raze?"

"Wasp."

"And the girls?"

"Somebody new. Name's Tally." He looked at his phone, shook his head, and put it in his pocket. "She'll be working at the school as an aide."

"Thanks, bro."

He put his hands on my shoulders. "Keep your eyes open. Be aware of what's going on around you. No leaving your doors unlocked or sitting out on your deck."

"Stop. I won't be a prisoner in my own home."

"Just until we figure out where Cliff is going to land."

"Do you have someone on Ava and Sam?"

"Damn right, I do."

"Who?"

"Bunker."

I smiled. The guy was a beast. Not that Wasp was a lightweight.

"Wasp won't fly with you. When you're gone, he'll work with Tally."

Of the three people my brother mentioned, Tally was the only one I hadn't met or gotten to know. "When's Cliff getting out?"

"Tomorrow."

—Monk—

"We're going to miss you, Mr. Yáñez," said the head nurse who was typically on days.

"No offense, Steph, but I'm not gonna miss this place."

"No offense taken. We all wish you the absolute best."

Hospital policy was that patients were to be taken to the front door in a wheelchair, but as hard as Onyx had worked in the last four months to walk again, no one mentioned policy. I arranged for a driver to transport us to my loft, where Onyx would be living for the time being. At least until he got cleared to fly again.

"Nice place," he said when I unlocked the door. "Surprised you didn't spend more time here."

I walked over to the refrigerator and got out two beers. I opened one and handed it to him. It wasn't like I hadn't sneaked plenty into the hospital, but I guessed it felt a hell of a lot different to be able to have one without anyone watching, anyone caring, or anyone looking the other way.

"This is you," I said, showing Onyx to the master bedroom.

"I'm not taking your room, son."

"I don't sleep in here."

"Why not?"

"Just don't."

Onyx threw his bag on the bed and kicked off his shoes. "Goddamn, it's gonna feel good not to have someone waking me up all the fucking time to take my blood pressure." He looked up at me. "You aren't gonna do that, are you?"

I shook my head, walked back out to the kitchen, and pulled out a box of prepackaged meal kits. Most days, I worked out so hard alongside Onyx that I was too tired to cook like I used to, but I'd gotten so sick of eating out.

Between eating healthier and working out with Onyx every day, I'd gotten bigger and leaner. I felt like my skin fit better. I wished it was as easy to work the shit out of my brain as it was my body. I still thought about Saylor all day and night. Everything, even things that had no logical reason for reminding me of her, did.

"All right, son, why the hell does that big ol' bed in there sit empty every night?"

"It just does."

"What happened between you and Saylor?"

"Didn't work out."

"Tell you what. I'll make a deal with you."

"Not interested."

"You don't know what I'm going to say."

I shook my head. Whatever it was, I was certain it involved telling Onyx about Saylor, and that wasn't something I was willing to do.

"I'm gonna tell you anyway, cuz we aren't gonna do this tonight."

I got a skillet out of the cupboard and unwrapped two pieces of salmon.

"I can hear your agreement from across the room."

I laughed and shook my head. "As I said, not interested."

"I'm gonna tell you what happened with Corazón, and you're gonna tell me what happened with Saylor, and if you don't agree to this, there ain't anybody ever gonna know what happened in that fuckin' cockpit."

I turned the fire off on the stove, got two more beers out of the fridge, and walked over to where Onyx stood on the patio I'd never gone out on.

"There's nothing to tell. It just didn't work out."

"Not what Razor said."

"Fuck," I mumbled under my breath, which made Onyx laugh.

"That's what I thought. We'll start tomorrow."

We didn't. After polishing off another six-pack, we started that night. Somehow, I ended up going first.

"Why didn't she tell you that she was flying?"

I shrugged. "Fuck if I know."

"Next question. Why did it bother you so much that she didn't?"

It was a question I'd asked myself a thousand times.

"I mean you don't tell anyone jack shit, so I'd say that's a little hypocritical."

"I have good reasons for not telling people what I'm doing. It's my job."

Onyx got up and walked into the kitchen. "We're outta beer, son. What else you got?"

"Bottle of Hennessy above the fridge."

"That's what I'm talkin' about. Damn. Why didn't we start with this shit?"

Onyx handed me a glass and sat back down.

"You know her ex is out of prison, right?"

My head shot up. "Who told you that?"

"Who do you think?"

"Who, Onyx?"

"Settle down. Razor did. He's got Wasp on her detail."

"He's a good man."

"Damn straight. Smart as shit too. Kinda like Saylor is."

Onyx's reference to Saylor's intelligence didn't go unnoticed. I got what he was up to. And it worked. In fact, it worked as soon as Onyx said the man's name. Wasp wasn't my main concern, though.

Saylor's ex was out of prison, which meant she was at risk, no matter who was on her detail. So were the girls and even Sally—anyone closely associated with Saylor and Razor.

"If it were me, I wouldn't be able to trust anyone else to protect my woman the way I would myself."

"Point made."

"What are you gonna do about it?"

"What the fuck do you think I'm going to do?"

30

I knew I came across as desperate, but I didn't care. I couldn't just sit in my house and wait to see if Cliff showed up. I had to get out of here.

I hadn't heard from Mantis, who I typically received my flight assignments from, but, God, I needed to get into the air. Not just me. I wanted my girls with me. And my mom. I wouldn't mind if Razor, Ava, and Sam came with us too.

"Jesus," I said out loud. Nothing like running away from my own life. Instead of hijacking K19's plane, I called Poppy.

"Hey, girlfriend. How the hell are you?"

"I'm okay. That isn't true. I'm ready to jump out of my skin. Did you hear Cliff's out?"

"*No!*"

"Yep. Today, I guess. Razor called in the National Guard, but it doesn't seem to be helping my nerves."

"Wait. What? He called in the National Guard?"

"The K19 version of it."

"Does that mean the elusive Monk is back in town?"

"No. Monk is still on the East Coast."

"I'm sorry, Saylor."

"I wish people would quit saying that to me. It's not like Monk Perrin is the last man on earth. Besides, I don't need a man to complete me, Poppy. I'm doing just fine on my own."

"You keep telling yourself that."

"You're single. Do you feel like less of a person because you haven't met the man who 'completes' you yet?"

"First of all, thank you for adding 'yet.' Second, this isn't about being single or in a relationship. This is about you and Monk. He is the person who completes you. That's the difference."

"He doesn't agree."

"Same bullshit, Saylor. What you two need is a month on a deserted island where you'd be forced to communicate with each other to survive."

"He's moved on; so have I."

"He has? He's seeing someone else? I can't believe it!"

"That isn't what I meant. I just meant he's…moved on."

"Got it. Anyway, enough about the quiet one. My guess is you called to talk about something else."

"I was wondering if you'd be interested in a road trip this weekend."

"Get outta Dodge? You know I'm always up for that. Are the doodlebugs coming with us? What about Ya-Ya?"

"You read my mind."

"Where are we going?"

"I was thinking Manzanita. If it would be okay. We could always stay in a hotel."

"It's perfect, actually. My parents are in Europe for a month, and if they weren't, they wouldn't be at the beach this early. Still too cold for them even though they've lived on the Oregon Coast all their lives. Are we taking two cars?"

"Caravan actually."

"Right."

"So, we'll leave Friday after the girls are out of school?"

"Can't wait. We need a getaway, even if we're bringing an entourage with us."

"Shit." I looked out the window as I closed the blinds.

"What?"

"It looks like someone is out on the trail in front of the house."

"It's probably just a member of your security team."

I half laughed. Poppy was probably right. No way in hell Cliff would be so bold. He knew what my brother did for a living.

—Monk—

I dumped the rest of the cognac in my glass in the sink. If I was going to be traveling in the morning, I needed to stop drinking now.

Onyx, who had gone into the bedroom, came back out. "Yeah, he's right here," he said, handing his cell to me.

"Hello?"

"I hear you need transport to the West Coast tomorrow."

"I thought you were grounded," I said to Alegria.

She laughed. "Only by choice. My parents are in town. Between them and Mantis' mother and father, Ian is well cared for. I need to fly, Monk."

"Just tell me when and where."

A few minutes later, Alegria sent a text telling me to meet her and her father, who would fly with us, at Potomac Airfield at zero eight hundred hours. By mid-afternoon tomorrow, I'd be back in Oregon.

I'd heard about the Cirrus jet, but had never been on one. Besides the pilot and co-pilot, the aircraft had room for five additional passengers. With a two-million-dollar price tag, it didn't lack any luxury. I wasn't sure if it was a rumor, but I'd heard the plane had a whole-aircraft parachute system.

"Yes, it does," answered Alegria when I asked. "Let's hope we never have to use it."

I rested my head back against the leather seat and closed my eyes. I had no idea how Saylor would react when I arrived. Onyx had made it abundantly clear that he thought I handled the whole pilot issue like a jackass, and she likely agreed.

No matter what she thought about me at this point, I couldn't leave her and her daughters' safety in anyone else's hands. Saylor might not want anything to do with me, and that would have to be okay. I'd still be part of her detail.

Instead of taking the Jeep to Manzanita, Razor insisted we caravan with two of K19's SUVs. Part of me felt like it was overkill, but if my brother believed there was a potential risk, I had to respect that.

The girls' bags were packed and in the garage, ready to go. I was wheeling my suitcase out of the bedroom when I heard a knock at the door.

I tried to shake off the pinpricks of fear that coursed through my body, reminding myself that I wouldn't allow Cliff to have this power over me.

My resolve was instantly quashed when I rounded the corner to find him standing on my deck. I quickly turned around, praying he hadn't seen me, and called Razor.

"Cliff is here," I said, my voice barely above a whisper.

"Goddammit. What is he doing? The restraining order is still in place."

"What am I supposed to do now?"

"Hang tight, kiddo. I'm already on my way. You stay put. Where's your gun?"

"In the safe in the closet."

"Get it out, Saylor, but do not leave that room until you hear from me."

I heard the familiar tone of the call ending and went to the closet to open the safe like Razor told me to do. I sat on the edge of the bed, facing the door, gun in hand, watching the minutes tick by on my bedside clock and listening to the deafening silence.

When my phone rang ten minutes later, I almost jumped out of my skin.

"Hi, Raze."

"All clear, sis. You can put the gun away and come on out."

"Do I want to know what happened?"

I heard the three tones again indicating the call had ended. That was rude, and I intended to tell my brother so.

Once my gun was safely back in the safe, I wiped my sweaty palms on my jeans and rolled my shoulders.

When I walked outside, I could see Razor on the deck. It looked like he was talking to someone, but I couldn't see who.

"Quit hanging up on me," I said, opening the door and walking out.

I turned my head, expecting to see Wasp. Instead, it was Monk.

I looked between him and my brother. "Hi."

Razor walked down the steps that led to the trail and squeezed Monk's shoulder as he passed by. "See ya later, Saylor," he said, waving behind him.

"What's going on?" I asked with one hand on my hip. It occurred to me at that moment that my stance was exactly the same as my daughter's when she did the same thing.

"Can we go inside?" he asked.

I backed up to allow Monk to walk in first, but he stepped behind me and held the door.

"What are you doing here?"

"I heard your ex was out of prison."

"He was here. What happened?"

"We missed him."

I felt sick to my stomach. "There should be security footage."

"Yes. That alone should show he violated the terms of his parole." Monk stood in front of me and cupped my cheek with his palm.

I shook my head and took a step back. "You didn't answer my question. What are you doing here?"

"I'm part of your detail."

"Why didn't anyone tell me?"

"No one knew."

I pulled a chair out from the dining room table and sat down. "I get that you don't like to talk, Monk, but my ex-husband, who may or may not be a loose cannon, was just standing on the deck of the house where my two daughters and I live. My brother told me to hide out in the bedroom and get my gun out. Adrenaline is coursing through my veins, and the last thing I want to do is play twenty questions with you. If you could just lay it all out for me, I'd really appreciate it. If you can't—or won't—you should just leave."

Monk pulled out a chair like I had and sat down. "Onyx got out of the hospital the same day your ex-husband was paroled."

I folded my arms and sat back in the chair.

"He's the one who told me. I got on a plane the next morning, and once I landed, I've been keeping an eye on things."

"An eye on things?" I shook my head. "When did you get here?"

"Three days ago."

"You said no one knew."

"That's right."

"Wasp didn't know?"

"Negative."

"That doesn't thrill me. If he didn't know you were here, I guess that explains how Cliff was able to get so close."

Given Monk's scowl, he agreed.

I studied him. "If that's all you have to tell me, you should leave." I pushed the chair back and stood.

Monk grasped my wrist and pulled me back down. "Please."

"Please, what, Monk?" I weaved my fingers in my hair and rested my elbows on the table. "I can't do this."

He put his hand on my arm. "Look at me."

I turned my head. "If you have something else to say, say it. I'm finished talking."

Monk looked into my eyes long enough that I was certain he was going to remain silent. Just as I went to stand a second time, he cleared his throat.

"There isn't anyone I trust with your safety." He leaned forward. "Not Wasp, not anyone."

"Not my brother?"

"Not your brother. And before you say anything, I can guarantee you that he'd say the same thing about Ava."

I knew Monk was right; Razor wouldn't be able to let go of control when it came to the safety of his pregnant wife and child.

"What will happen to Cliff?"

"He violated the terms of his parole, which means he should go back to prison."

"Should?"

"I believe Razor is working with the sheriff's department to get him picked up."

"I don't like living this way."

"We need to work out some things between us."

I stood, and this time, Monk didn't try to stop me. I walked over and looked out the kitchen window. "My friend Poppy said we should be forced to live on a deserted island for a month where we'd have to communicate in order to stay alive."

Monk stood too, reached out, and touched my cheek. "I like the deserted island part."

I turned around to look at him. "To be honest, so do I."

"I have a question for you."

"If you're going to ask why I didn't tell you that I was getting my pilot's license, I don't have an answer."

"Try, Saylor."

"Sorry to bring up Poppy again, but she asked if the reason I didn't tell you about flying was because I was afraid you'd try to talk me out of it."

"Why would you think I would do that?"

"I didn't say I did. I said Poppy suggested that as a possible reason."

"Is there any truth to it?"

I turned again and looked out the window. "I don't like to think of myself as a trite person, Monk, but why didn't you tell me you were back in the States and staying in Washington, DC, with Onyx? You've been here three days. Why didn't you tell me you were here?" I held up my hand when he took a deep breath. "Rhetorical questions, Monk. I'm not looking for an answer. In fact, I don't want one."

"As you said with Poppy, I'm sorry to bring up Onyx again, but like you, he accused me of hypocrisy."

"He was right."

I looked over my shoulder; Monk was smiling.

"The girls and I are going to Manzanita with my mom and Poppy. We're leaving this afternoon."

"Razor mentioned the trip."

"What will you do?"

"I'm not certain yet."

"I have things to do to get ready."

Monk reached out and put his hand on the small of my back. I didn't shrug it away, but I didn't turn to him either. My emotions were all over the place, in part because of the overwhelming fear I felt when I'd seen Cliff right outside my door, but also because Monk was here.

It would be too easy to turn to him, let him comfort me, only to have him walk out of my life over and over again. It wasn't just his job. That was something else Poppy was right about. Razor had worked it out so he wasn't gone all the time. He wasn't the only one. Doc and Merrigan were married with a family; it was the same with Gunner and Raketa. Hell, most of the K19 team was married and either had children or they were on the way.

If they could figure it out, so could Monk. The difference was, he didn't want to. He was perfectly comfortable living a life separate from mine, only dropping in when it suited him.

It was better not to be in any relationship versus one that left me feeling as though I wasn't important enough to make an effort for.

I turned and put my hand on his cheek. "I care about you, Monk, and I wish you every happiness, but I can't let you waltz in and out of my life. It isn't about the girls at this point. I know that I've used them as an excuse in the past, wanting to protect them from hurt. This, though, is all about me." I leaned forward, touched my lips to his, walked past him to the door, and opened it. "Goodbye, Monk."

—Monk—

I hesitated only momentarily. What I heard in Saylor's voice was different than any other time she'd said goodbye to me. This time, there was no ambivalence, no room for talking it out. I didn't touch her on my way out, didn't try to kiss her, didn't even look into her eyes. "Goodbye, Saylor."

I was off the deck before the door closed, and I didn't look back.

"How'd it go?" Razor asked when I walked into the office.

"With?"

He spun around in his chair. "My sister, asshole."

"Fine."

"Right," he said, returning to whatever he was working on.

"We need to talk about her detail."

"You freelancing on this one, Monk, or are you part of the team?"

My first inclination was to walk out, but Razor was right to call me out. I was part of a team; I was a partner. Going off on my own, not letting anyone know I was here, was a jackass move on my part.

"I shouldn't have handled it the way I did."

"That's a start."

"Meaning?"

"You've written your own game plan since the plane crash, and no one has said a word to you about it. We've operated this firm with a missing piece, without any idea when you might get yourself back to work. Not to mention, you've been drawing a salary the entire time."

"Are you asking me to resign?"

Razor's jaw tightened. "Did you hear me ask you to resign?"

"Negative."

"Look, I'm the last person you should be talking to about this, because for me, it's personal. I'm mad as hell at you for the way you've treated my sister. She's the most giving, caring, loving person I know other than Avarie and my mom. Before you ask, she hasn't talked to me about you, and she never will, but I have eyes. I can see her hurt."

"I'm sorry."

Razor stood and faced me. "Yeah? For what? Not pulling your head out of your ass and either stepping up to the plate or walking away? Either would've worked.

Hanging out somewhere in the middle with no regard for anyone but yourself doesn't work."

When Razor walked out and went upstairs, I sat in the vacated chair. I'd gotten several dressing downs over the course of my career, but none had as big of an impact as the one I'd just received. And yet, here I sat with no idea what to do next. Finally, I pulled out my phone and called Doc.

"Been waiting to hear from you," the man said when he answered. Was his voice as clipped as Razor's had been, or was it my imagination?

"I'd like to meet."

"When?"

"As soon as possible."

"Coincidentally, Merrigan and I aren't far from you. We should arrive at the Overleaf in a couple of hours."

32

"There's a delay. You can't leave until tomorrow," said my brother when he walked into my kitchen.

"The girls only have two days off, Raze. There's no point in going if we can't leave this afternoon."

"I don't want them going to school anyway, at least until Cliff is back in custody."

I looked over my shoulder. The girls' bedroom door was closed, but I didn't want to risk them overhearing the conversation we were having. I led him out to the deck.

"I told you I won't live my life like a prisoner. I won't do that to them either."

"Have a seat."

I put my hand on my hip and then took it off. I really needed to stop doing that. "No."

"Jesus, Saylor. Please sit down."

I did, but I wasn't happy about it. Razor pulled a chair out and spun it around. Why did guys do that? Couldn't he just sit on the chair the right way?

"I want you to close your eyes for a minute."

"No. I'm not a child, Razor. Say whatever is on your mind."

"I will not be able to live with myself if anything happens to you or my nieces because I didn't listen to my gut. Right now, it's telling me that Cliff is a threat. A serious threat. Maybe I'm wrong, but I don't ever second-guess myself. I need to make some changes in your detail, and I can't do that in the next hour."

"What happened to Wasp?"

Razor scrubbed his face with his hand, and I stood up.

"Tell me what happened."

"Tally called for backup, and that's where he was. He and Cliff likely crossed paths."

I sat back down when I felt my legs give out. "He was at the school."

"Yes. I'm sorry, sis."

"We're leaving. Not just to Manzanita."

"I understand that reaction, but I still need time to put a bigger team together."

"You know that thing I said about not being a prisoner? I won't be a sitting duck either."

"Give me until tomorrow morning."

"What about Monk?"

"He's meeting with Doc and Merrigan now at the Overleaf."

I didn't know they were in town, not that I needed to. "Is he leaving K19?"

"I don't know."

—Monk—

I didn't have to be at the Overleaf for another hour, but I got on the bike anyway. I needed to settle my thoughts. My mind had raced since I'd talked to Doc, and I still hadn't come up with anything definitive to discuss, except to own up to everything Razor said earlier, take responsibility for my actions, and suffer the consequences.

I had had my head up my ass, and no one had called me out on it until today. I hadn't bothered to discuss my plan to stay in DC; I made the decision to do it and never looked back. What more could I do than offer my *mea culpa* and see what happened from there?

I rode south along the ocean for thirty miles and then turned around and rode back.

As I parked the bike, I saw a familiar-looking black SUV pull up to the inn's entrance. Merrigan got out of the vehicle first and went inside; Doc walked over to where I was.

"It's good to see you," Doc said, putting his hand on my shoulder. "It's been a rough few months. Let's go inside."

"What brings you to Oregon?" I asked as I followed him into the lobby.

"There's a firm in Portland interested in hiring K19 for private security. We wanted to see their outfit in person before we came to an agreement." Doc motioned to the sofa and two chairs inside an alcove where we could talk privately.

"Have a seat. I'll see if I can round up something to drink. What would you like?"

"Water would be good, thanks."

"Hello, Monk," said Merrigan. I stood and we embraced. "How are you?"

"Hanging in there. How are you?"

She motioned for me to take a seat. "We're also hanging in there. I sometimes think my work with MI6 was far easier than knowing how to properly parent two wee ones, both with minds of their own. However, please know I'm not complaining."

She gazed up at Doc when he came in with a pitcher of water and three glasses.

"Thanks," I said when he handed me a glass and then sat down next to his wife.

"Kade tells me you wanted to meet. What would you like to discuss?" Merrigan asked, folding her hands on her lap.

"It's been brought to my attention that I haven't been living up to the obligations I agreed to when I became a K19 partner. I want you to know I take full responsibility."

"The circumstances have been extenuating," she responded, looking at Doc.

"It doesn't excuse the fact that I made decisions without consulting you and have continued to do so."

"We all understood," she said. "If we hadn't, we would've asked."

"If you still want me on the team, I'm ready to get back to work."

Merrigan leaned forward. "You are part of the team, Monk. There isn't any question of that. We're more than a team, though. We're family. Onyx is part of our family, and you did what you thought best for him."

"There's more."

Merrigan raised a brow and looked over at Doc again. "Saylor?"

"I've been back in Oregon since Tuesday, but no one knew that."

Merrigan laughed, and so did Doc. "Everyone knew that, Monk. You flew with Alegria."

"I'm going to jump in here if no one objects," said Doc, not waiting for either his wife or I to respond. "Razor has a bug up his ass, but it isn't because of you. In his mind, he failed his sister, first by not making sure her ex-husband didn't get paroled, and then when Cliff got so close to both Saylor and her daughters."

"But I—"

"I'm not finished. I spoke to Razor on our way here. Let me fill you in on what is presently taking place. Later this afternoon, we'll be leaving for Montecito. Saylor, her daughters, and Sally are going with us and will stay with us until Cliff is apprehended. You, Wasp, and Tally will remain on their detail until further notice, and you are the lead. Understood?"

"Yes, sir."

Doc got up. "Good. Now, if you'll excuse me."

"Monk, I'm going to speak to you now as a woman and a friend rather than as managing partner of K19,"

Merrigan said as Doc walked over to the bank of elevators. "You don't have to respond. All I ask is that you hear me out."

"Yes, ma'am."

"You're at the same crossroads many of us have found ourselves at in the last few years. Perhaps, like me, you never thought being in a long-term relationship was possible, given your line of work. Maybe it had nothing to do with your choice of career, but it still wasn't something you believed was possible."

My gaze never wavered; she'd asked me to hear her out, and I intended to do so.

"I will say only this. It's possible, Monk. What's more is, it's worth it."

I took a deep breath and exhaled slowly. Did Merrigan know how hard her words were hitting?

"When I say the K19 team is a family, those aren't just words," she added. "We care about each other just as much as if we were related by blood. It isn't solely about the mission; it's about the lives we lead. You did nothing wrong when you made a commitment to stay with your *brother* Onyx as he recovered. You did nothing wrong when you left DC because you were concerned about Saylor's safety. Do you have any questions, Monk?"

"Doc said I'm the lead on Saylor's detail?"

"That's right."

"I should be with her."

She smiled. "I agree."

33

—Saylor—

After my brother left, I stayed out on the deck a few more minutes. The idea that Cliff had been at the girls' school bothered me far more than him showing up at the house. I took a deep breath, knowing I needed to do a better job of masking my fear before I went inside to talk to Sierra and Savannah about our change of plans.

Razor's response when I asked if Monk was leaving K19 added to my overall anxiety. Whether we were in a relationship or not, there was never anyone else who made me feel as safe as Monk did, not even my brother. If he did leave, I prayed he'd at least come and say a final goodbye.

I stood and stretched, rolling my shoulders to ease the tension in them, and went inside.

"Hello, Saylor."

I looked up at the sound of my ex-husband's voice. The man was standing in my kitchen.

"How did you get in here?"

He took a step in my direction. "That's not important."

"There's a restraining order—"

"Fuck the restraining order. I want to see my daughters."

I held my breath, hoping neither of my girls came out of the bedroom to see who was in the kitchen, yelling at their mother.

"Go get them." When he motioned toward the hallway, I saw he held a gun in his hand.

"Cliff, that isn't necessary. Please put the gun away. I'll get the girls. Just please, I beg you, don't hurt them."

"You think I'd hurt them?" he seethed. "It's you I'll hurt, not them. Now go!"

"You're going to frighten them."

"Not if you do as I asked. Go get them now and tell them there's someone you want them to meet. And, Saylor, I'll be right around the corner, listening to every word you say, so don't try anything stupid."

He was close enough that I could feel the gun against my back. I walked toward the door, trying to decide if I should open it or turn around and try to get the weapon away from him. I might die in the process, and then I wouldn't be here to protect my daughters. I put my hand on the knob, and it felt cold. Why would it be cold?

I slowly opened the door and crept inside. The window was wide open, and I didn't see either of the girls.

I turned around to look in their walk-in closet and saw Monk instead, standing just inside, holding a gun in one hand and the finger of his other hand to his lips.

My eyes opened wide as he pulled me toward him, into the closet, and motioned for me to get down. "Gun," I whispered as quietly as I could, praying Cliff wouldn't hear me.

"What the fuck do we have here?" I heard Cliff say a few seconds later. I couldn't see around Monk, but it sounded like Cliff was walking toward the open window. "Stupid bitch," he muttered.

"Drop your gun and keep your hands where I can see them!" I heard Monk shout. I closed my eyes and held my breath, knowing that in the next couple of seconds one or both of them would shoot.

"Do it!" Monk shouted again. A split second later, I heard the gunshot I'd anticipated. Only one, and Monk was still standing.

"Saylor, stay where you are," he said as he walked into the room. I peeked through the open door and saw my ex-husband's body on the floor. Monk kicked the gun Cliff had dropped away and then knelt down.

"He's dead, Saylor, but I'm warning you, this isn't something you want to see," Monk said at the same time I heard people running in the hall in our direction.

"Where is she?" I heard my brother ask.

"Closet," Monk answered. "Get her out of here. Don't let her see this."

Razor helped me up and put his arm around me. "Monk is right, sweetheart. Close your eyes, and I'll guide you out of the room."

Even if Razor hadn't told me to, I would've closed them anyway. I'd seen one dead body in my life—my father's after he'd had a heart attack. It still haunted me; I didn't need to see another.

"Where are my girls?" I asked as Razor led me out of the room and down the hallway.

"They're safe."

I stopped walking. "Tell me where they are," I shouted at him.

"They're at your brother's house with Merrigan," said Doc, walking toward us. "Come with me. I'll take you to them." Doc kept his arm firmly around my shoulders.

"Where's my mother?"

"She's with them. Everyone is safe. No one was hurt."

"Cliff is dead."

"Yes, he is, and you're safe."

—Monk—

I was within a foot of Saylor and Doc when I saw her legs give out.

"Let me," I said, racing forward and taking her in my arms.

"She's out. You got her?" Doc asked.

I held her close to me.

"Take her to Razor's. I'll help with cleanup."

I walked slowly down the trail and up the front steps of her brother's house. Before I could get the door open, she came to.

"What happened?" she asked.

"You fainted," I said as Merrigan opened the door to let us in.

I set her on her feet when I saw Sierra and Savannah racing over. Neither said a word as Saylor nestled them in her arms like I'd done to her.

"I love you both so much," I heard her murmur.

"We love you too, Mama," the girls answered with their arms tight around their mother's neck.

I knelt down next to them and brushed a tear from Saylor's cheek. "Can I get in on this?"

Sierra let go of her mother and put her arm around my neck instead. I didn't know how long we stayed that way, but just as my legs began to ache from the position I was in, Sierra let go. I stood and helped Saylor do the same.

"Where is everyone?" she asked, looking around the empty room.

"Mama, what happened?" asked Savannah, whose lower lip was quivering. "We were in our room, and Miss Tally said we had to climb out the window and come with her, and then Mr. Monk was carrying you, and…"

Saylor picked Savannah up as her little girl dissolved into tears. When I put my arm around Sierra's shoulders, she turned into me and cried as hard as her sister was. I knelt down and brushed her tears away.

"Everything is okay," I murmured when she wrapped her arms around my neck.

"What happened?" I heard her whisper.

"We can talk about all that later. I bet your mama would like a glass of water," I said. "What about you?"

Sierra let go of my neck, grasped my hand instead, and walked toward the kitchen. "She might like that better," she said, pointing to the bottle of wine on the counter.

I laughed. "You're probably right. We'll give her both."

"She is right," said Saylor, walking in with Savannah, who immediately went to help her sister get water from the fridge.

When I opened my arms, Saylor walked into them.

"Thank you," she whispered.

I brought her as close to my body as I could. "We need to talk about tonight."

Saylor turned her head so her cheek rested on my chest. I could feel the warmth of her breath on my skin. "What about it?"

"We're having a sleepover. Even if I have to sleep on the couch."

"Just tonight?"

I shook my head. "Every night."

"Then, you better not sleep on the couch."

34

"They're going to be fine, like they always are," said Poppy, rolling her eyes. "I have several other rooms in my house to paint if they get bored."

"I know. It's just a long time to be away from them. It's a lot on you too."

"You need to do this, and it isn't just me. Ya-Ya is taking the second two weeks."

I looked over and saw Monk smiling at me. "What?"

"We don't have to go for the whole month."

"Yes, we do."

"Come here."

I walked over and sat on his lap.

"What happened to the no-PDA rule?" asked Poppy when Monk kissed me.

"We got rid of that at the same time as the no-sleepover rule." I kissed him again.

"Okay, then, I'm outta here. I'll see you in the morning."

Monk moved me off his lap, got up, and locked the door after Poppy left.

"I meant what I said. We can cut the number of days we're gone."

"Absolutely not. We agreed on a month."

Monk cupped my cheek. "We don't even have to leave Yachats, not if we both agree that I won't take on any missions and you won't take on any flights."

"Merrigan wouldn't schedule us anyway. And, no, we need this time, Monk."

"I'll pick up the girls after my meeting."

"Are you sure?"

"You promised to make pizza, and you know I love your pizza." He snaked his arm around my waist. "I love everything about you, Saylor."

"We'll see."

Monk laughed, kissed me one more time, and left through the garage. He wasn't gone five minutes before my mom came over.

"Are you getting excited for your trip?"

"Excited. Nervous. Same difference, right?"

She sat down on the stool by the kitchen counter. "What are you nervous about?"

"A whole month, Mom. What if I get on his nerves and he decides he doesn't love me after all?"

"You can't be serious," she said, raising a brow.

I got out the mixer, set it on the counter, and began collecting ingredients for the pizza.

"Can I help?"

"You didn't think I was just going to let you sit there and do nothing, did you?"

My mom laughed while she washed her hands. "Tell me the truth. You aren't really nervous, are you?"

"Yes and no. We've never spent this much time together."

"Tell me where you're staying again."

"Meeta-Rah. It's a resort on a small island in the Laccadive Sea."

"A private island?"

"Not completely, no. Although Monk did say we don't have to see any other people if we don't want to. We have our own villa."

She shook her head. "Your father took me to Canada once."

I laughed. "I'm sorry, Mom."

My mom pulled me into a hug. "Don't be. I'm happy for you, sweetheart. I'm glad you decided to open your heart again."

"I think Monk would've worked his way in even if it was closed."

—Monk—

"Want a beer?" Razor asked.

"No, thanks. I'm picking the girls up from school after I leave here."

He clapped my shoulder. "You're a good man, Perrin."

I followed him out onto the deck. "I'm going to ask your sister to marry me."

"About damn time," said Razor, taking a swig of beer.

"So you approve?"

"If I didn't, you wouldn't be around to ask."

"I love her. I love the girls too."

"Are you planning to adopt them?"

"I'd like to, but first I have to talk your sister into spending the rest of her life with me."

"I don't think it'll be a hard sell, my friend."

"I have another question."

"Shoot."

"What about the girls? Should I tell them? Ask them?"

"If they want to be adopted?"

I shook my head. "If I can marry their mother."

The smile left Razor's face, and he turned away.

"I guess that's a 'no.'"

"Wrong. That's a 'I don't want you to see how emotional I got when you said that.'"

"I gotta go."

"Wait." Razor looked at his phone. "What time does school get out?"

"Three, but I've got a stop to make."

"To get a ring?"

"Flowers."

When the bell rang, I was waiting on the front steps of the elementary school. I never waited in the car line. That was no way to pick up two little girls at the end of a long day. Plus, I loved seeing their faces when they came out and saw me waiting with both arms behind my back.

"What do you have for us today, Mr. Monk?" asked Savannah, running ahead of her sister.

"That isn't polite. You didn't even say hello."

Savannah stuck her tongue out at Sierra.

"You know your mother doesn't like that," I said, scrunching my eyes.

"I'm sorry," she said, looking at the ground.

"It isn't me you need to apologize to. Say it to your sister."

Once she had, I told them both to close their eyes. "Okay, open."

"Bouquets? They're so pretty!" exclaimed Sierra.

"They're like the ones we had for Aunt Ava's wedding."

I laughed. Everything was always Aunt Ava, never Uncle Razor.

I led them farther off the sidewalk and knelt down. "I have something very important to ask you."

With wide eyes, both girls nodded. "Go ahead, Mr. Monk," said Sierra.

"While we're on our trip, I'm going to ask your mother to marry me. If that's okay with the two of you."

Savannah's eyes lit up, and she shoved the flowers closer to me. "Are these for when we're flower girls?"

"Those are to practice with." I looked between them. "But you haven't answered me."

"Of course it's okay." Savannah put her arms around my neck. Sierra, though, held back, studying her flowers. I reached out and took her hand.

"I wouldn't just be marrying your mom. In a way, I'd be marrying both of you too. We'd be a family."

Sierra's eyes filled with tears.

"Tell me why you're crying, sweetheart."

She stepped forward and leaned into me. "Will you be our dad?" she asked.

"If you want me to, absolutely."

"Can we call you that?" Savannah asked.

"Dad? I don't see why not, but we have to ask your mom first, okay?"

"We can't until they get back from their trip," Sierra told her sister.

"Why not?" I asked.

She shook her head. "If you're going to propose, you have to plan something special. And it can't be when she's making pizza."

"Yeah, Mr. Monk, that wouldn't be good," said Savannah with a grim look on her face.

Epilogue

"Where should we go on our honeymoon?" Monk asked on our flight back from the Maldives.

"Honeymoon? That wasn't it?" I looked down at the beautiful diamond ring he'd given me when he proposed on our last night on the island.

"Somewhere we can take the girls."

I rested my head on Monk's shoulder. "I can't believe they kept so mum the night before we left."

"They didn't think I should propose while you were making pizza."

"Too many princess movies I guess."

Monk kissed me. "I'm glad you said yes."

"Did you really think there was a chance I wouldn't? Is that why you waited until the last night?"

"I promised you a month on a deserted island, remember?"

"We did get pretty good at communicating."

Monk dipped his finger into the top of my sundress and traced the outline of where the lace of my bra met my skin. "Not necessarily by talking."

"You talked plenty. Now, we need to practice more kissing.

Keep reading for a sneak peek
at the next book
in the K19 Security Solutions
Team Two series,
HALO'S OATH!

Prologue

Halo

Tara came around to where I was cooking. "Um, I think you might want to turn the heat down a little."

Heat? Down? What did she say? I looked at the pan in front of me and at the edges of the vegetables that were turning black. "Oh. Right." I turned the burner off.

She laughed. "What just happened?"

"Flashbacks," I said, pointing to the counter with my spatula.

"Yeah?" she asked, looking down at where my rock-hard cock strained my zipper.

"Sorry," I mumbled.

"Tell you what. You give me a taste, and I'll reciprocate."

I looked up at her, and she motioned with her head to the pan. "A mushroom, please."

I grabbed a fork, speared one, and brought it to her mouth.

"Mmm. That tastes so good. Your turn. What do you want to try?"

Was she really saying what I thought she was? Unable to speak, I motioned to her tits with the fork.

"This?" she asked, pointing where I had.

I nodded. Maybe I grunted. I know I groaned when she pulled her shirt over her head and I saw her breasts were bare beneath it.

I put one arm around her back and leaned forward, getting as much of her tit in my mouth as I could. I swirled my tongue around her nipple. Tara weaved her fingers in my hair, and when I went to move to the other breast, she pulled.

"Uh-uh. My turn."

I stood and, since I'd suddenly gone mute, pointed at the pan of veggies.

"A pepper, please."

I speared it and brought it to her mouth. She chewed it slowly, making the same sound she had when she tasted the wine. Her eyes, instead of rolling back in her head, stayed fixed on mine.

She motioned with her hands to her boobs, but I had a different idea. Instead of going for seconds, I brought my lips to her mouth.

"Oh my God," I moaned, finally finding my voice. "You taste so…damn…good." I cupped her face with both my hands and pressed against her lips with my tongue, thrusting inside when she opened to me. When I angled my head and went deeper, Tara wrapped her arms around my neck.

I reached down and put both hands on her ass, lifting until her legs went around my waist.

"What do you want a taste of now, baby?"

She plastered her mouth against mine and kissed me as hard as I'd kissed her. After a few moments of dueling tongues, I pulled back. "Does this mean it's my turn again?"

"Mm-hmm."

I carried her around the counter and set her on her ass where I had the other night. Just like then, she leaned back, resting against the cool stone. I unfastened the button on her jeans and lowered the zipper.

Since it was my turn and I knew what I wanted to taste, I pulled her jeans and panties over her curves and down until they fell to the floor.

"Put your feet here," I said, lifting one and then the other so they rested on the edge of the counter. "Drop your knees."

Tara was spread out before me, and I intended not just to taste, but to eat my fill.

About the Author

USA Today and Amazon Top 15 Bestselling Author Heather Slade writes shamelessly sexy, edge-of-your seat romantic suspense.

She gave herself the gift of writing a book for her own birthday one year. Forty-plus books later (and counting), she's having the time of her life.

The women Slade writes are self-confident, strong, with wills of their own, and hearts as big as the Colorado sky. The men are sublimely sexy, seductive alphas who rise to the challenge of capturing the sweet soul of a woman whose heart they'll hold in the palm of their hand forever. Add in a couple of neck-snapping twists and turns, a page-turning mystery, and a swoon-worthy HEA, and you'll be holding one of her books in your hands.

She loves to hear from my readers. You can contact her at heather@heatherslade.com

To keep up with her latest news and releases, please visit her website at www.heatherslade.com to sign up for her newsletter.

MORE FROM AUTHOR HEATHER SLADE

BUTLER RANCH
Kade's Worth
Brodie's Promise
Maddox's Truce
Naughton's Secret
Mercer's Vow
Kade's Return
Butler Ranch Christmas

WICKED WINEMAKERS
FIRST LABEL
Brix's Bid
Ridge's Release
Press' Passion
Zin's Sins
Tryst's Temptation

WICKED WINEMAKERS
SECOND LABEL
Beau's Beloved
Coming Soon:
Cru's Crush
Bones' Bliss
Snapper's Seduction
Kick's Kiss

ROARING FORK RANCH
Coming Soon:
Roaring Fork Wrangler
Roaring Fork Roughstock
Roaring Fork Rockstar
Roaring Fork Rooker
Roaring Fork Bridger

THE ROYAL AGENTS
OF MI6
Make Me Shiver
Drive Me Wilder
Feel My Pinch
Chase My Shadow
Find My Angel

K19 SECURITY
SOLUTIONS TEAM ONE
Razor's Edge
Gunner's Redemption
Mistletoe's Magic
Mantis' Desire
Dutch's Salvation

K19 SECURITY
SOLUTIONS TEAM TWO
Striker's Choice
Monk's Fire
Halo's Oath
Tackle's Honor
Onyx's Awakening

K19 SHADOW OPERATIONS
TEAM ONE
Code Name: Ranger
Code Name: Diesel
Code Name: Wasp
Code Name: Cowboy
Code Name: Mayhem

K19 ALLIED INTELLIGENCE
TEAM ONE
Code Name: Ares
Code Name: Cayman
Code Name: Poseidon
Code Name: Zeppelin
Code Name: Magnet

K19 ALLIED INTELLIGENCE
TEAM TWO
Coming Soon:
Code Name: Puck
Code Name: Michelangelo
Code Name: Typhon
Code Name: Hornet
Code Name: Reaper

PROTECTORS
UNDERCOVER
Undercover Agent
Undercover Emissary
Coming Soon:
Undercover Savior
Undercover Infidel
Undercover Assassin

THE INVINCIBLES
TEAM ONE
Decked
Edged
Grinded
Riled
Smoked

THE INVINCIBLES
TEAM TWO
Bucked
Irished
Sainted
Hammered
Ripped

THE UNSTOPPABLES
TEAM ONE
Furied
Merried

COWBOYS OF
CRESTED BUTTE
A Cowboy Falls
A Cowboy's Dance
A Cowboy's Kiss
A Cowboy Stays
A Cowboy Wins